"It's all right. You're safe."

"What happened?" Samantha asked, her voice raspy.

"Tornado," Micah said, worry for his brother and sister increasing his anxiety. "Let's get you out of this car."

She tried to move then groaned before reaching her hand out. "Patch."

Micah checked her forehead. "You've got a bad bump. No patching needed."

"Patch," she said again, her voice frantic.

A dog barked and jumped into her lap.

"Is Patch your puppy?" Micah asked while he helped her out of the car. The little animal was lean and snarly and also frightened.

She looked at Micah, her expression full of fear and apprehension. "Yes," she said. "We're in trouble and we need your help."

She wobbled and fell into Micah's arms, the puppy shivering between them.

"You sure do need help," he said. "That was some storm."

The woman moaned again. "Not storm. Him. After me."

With over seventy books published and millions in print, **Lenora Worth** writes award-winning romance and romantic suspense. Three of her books finaled in the ACFW Carol Awards, and her Love Inspired Suspense novel *Body of Evidence* became a *New York Times* bestseller. Her novella in *Mistletoe Kisses* made her a *USA TODAY* bestselling author. Lenora goes on adventures with her retired husband, Don, and enjoys reading, baking and shopping...especially shoe shopping.

Visit the Author Profile page at Harlequin.com for more titles.

AMISH COUNTRY SECRET

LENORA WORTH

LOVE INSPIRED SUSPENSE

INSPIRATIONAL ROMANCE

ISBN-13: 9781335581075

Amish Country Secret

Copyright © 2021 by Lenora H. Nazworth

LOVE INSPIRED SUSPENSE

INSPIRATIONAL ROMANCE

LOVE INSPIRED°SUSPENSE
INSPIRATIONAL ROMANCE

ISBN-13: 978-1-335-58107-5

Amish Country Secret

And a man shall be as an hiding place from the wind, and a covert from the tempest; as rivers of water in a dry place, as the shadow of a great rock in a weary land.
—Isaiah 32:2

To those on the front lines—the fighters, the peaceful protestors, the marginalized and the overlooked, the military warriors and the everyday heroes and heroines who have to make the tough decisions.
I hope you find refuge in the storm.

ONE

A storm was coming.

Samantha Herndon had heard the radio reports all day long. Tornado watches, strong winds, possible tornadic damage. Seek shelter, stay safe. But she had much more to worry about.

Watching someone being murdered kind of outranked even the bad weather. Still in shock, she tried to get that horrible scene out of her head. But how could she? They knew she'd witnessed them killing that helpless homeless man.

And now *he* had sent someone after her.

She kept glancing back into the rearview mirror while a steady shiver moved down her spine. *He* was coming for her. A shiny black pickup truck had been following her since she'd turned off the main highway.

She'd been so careful, but he had ways of finding people. He'd always made that a joke between them. She'd never dreamed she'd get on his bad side.

Stay safe. She had to do that first. A few more miles and she could finally take a deep breath. That truck was probably going in the same direction.

So she kept driving, and prayed her old economy car would hold out. She had to get to Campton Creek before night set in. She could hide out there in the world she used to know. They'd never find her there. She prayed she'd gotten away before they'd realized she had escaped. They'd already figured out what she'd done, but she needed to get the evidence to someone who could help her.

When the tiny dog cuddling a blanket on the seat beside her whimpered, Samantha reached out a shaking hand to the scared little fellow. "It's okay, Patch. We'll be safe at Gramma's house."

The little black-and-white spotted dog looked up at her with trusting dark eyes, the black circle around one of those eyes the reason his now-dead owner had named him Patch. A mixed breed of Chihuahua and Jack Russell—a Jack Chi—the little dog had short silky hair and big ears. Samantha had fallen for him the minute she'd found him and recognized him. Patch was a keeper.

"If I hadn't found you wandering around, I would have never realized what's been going on right under my nose," she said, giving Patch another quick rub on his tiny head.

Samantha watched the sky, then checked the long road behind her. How had she managed to get caught up in such a web of evil?

Because she'd fallen for the wrong man. Years ago, she'd left her Amish community to return to her mother's side, but since then, she'd finished college and become a veterinarian. Some called her weird and some called her softhearted and over-the-top because she cared so much for innocent animals. This time, that caring trait had brought her Patch. It had also brought her face-to-face with the ugly truth.

She'd been caught between two worlds but she'd always known where her true home was—here with Gramma. Gramma wouldn't be at the house to meet her this time. Thankful that her gramma was off visiting her sister, Samantha checked the sky and tried to hurry the car along the winding road.

This trip would make Samantha an interloper, but this was the best place to hide out. He couldn't find her in her grandmother's small country home. Because she'd never told him she'd once lived here.

She looked into all the mirrors. The road behind her was empty. Maybe that truck had turned off. Maybe she was imagining things.

Patch leaned into her soft touch, some of his anxiety settling. Then his big ears perked up.

The wind changed and everything went still. Static hissed across the radio. Samantha hit the dash, trying to get the decrepit radio to work. Then she heard the sirens blaring through the little box.

Tornado warning. And from what she could hear, the storm was passing right over Campton Creek. She glanced in the mirror again and saw her worst nightmare.

The truck she'd seen earlier was real and the driver was barreling toward her as fast as the storm whirling over them. She saw the driver and another man on the passenger side of the huge vehicle. Had he tracked her from the moment she'd left upstate New York?

Samantha pushed her car to go faster along the curve of the narrow road that ribboned around the mountainside.

The wind held her back and the truck behind her came within inches of her vehicle. She made it down the mountain and looked back one last time.

The truck accelerated and came charging toward her. She didn't even have time to brace for the hit.

Bam! The force jarred her. Patch barked and almost fell off the seat.

"Hold on, Patch."

The big truck came again, harder this time. The hit sent her car spiraling into a spin. Samantha screamed, her hands clutching the steering wheel. When she heard the ominous sound that roared like a runaway freight train, Samantha felt almost thankful for the storm.

It might just save her from him.

Checking one more time in the rearview mirror, she gasped when she saw the pickup truck charging toward her again. This time he attempted to knock her car right off the road and into a deep ditch.

Samantha screamed and prepared for the crash, but suddenly the wind changed and the truck pulled back and to the right.

Panicked, she glanced in the mirror and watched as the truck behind her careened and trembled, wobbling like a top as it sailed over into the ditch and landed on its side. The wind had pitched the truck off the road.

Thank You, Lord.

That was her last thought before her car shifted and seemed to lift up like a toy in a giant's hands.

Micah King raced to get all the livestock inside the barn and make sure everything was locked down. The wind lifted and twisted the trees in a rage. Big drops of rain hit his face and arms. Small limbs and twigs swirled and swished by, pricking his skin.

His younger sister Emmie cried out from the house, running to meet him. "Micah, *kumm!*"

Micah ran toward the porch, the dark sky swirling around him. "Emmie, get inside. We have to go to the cellar. Where is Jed?"

"Already waiting by the cellar door," Emmie replied as Micah lifted her up. "He has supplies ready."

His sister's light weight made it easy, even if she would be twelve years old soon. Her twin brother, on the other hand, was almost as tall as Micah and always spoiling for a fight. At least he knew the tornado drill well enough to prepare.

Micah had Emmie almost to the back door when they heard a grinding sound. "Go," he shouted as he settled his sister, then turned to see the twirling vortex coming across the field. "Emmie, go with Jed into the cellar. I'll be there soon."

Another sound cracked against the roar of the angry storm. A crash of metal, a hiss of engines roaring. Then the booming sound of thunder and a collision.

To his amazement a bright red car came careening through the alfalfa field, tires grinding, gears protesting, chrome and metal flying away. The storm tossed the tiny vehicle like a leaf in the torrid gusts of angry wind and then slammed it down so hard it hit and landed at an odd angle. When he heard screams coming from the car, Micah slammed the door to the house shut and took off running in a sprint against the snarling wind.

Holding a hand over his eyes, debris passing like shrapnel all around him, he ducked down as the storm continued to increase. The sky roared like a piercing, grinding monster over his head while the sound of metal twisting and limbs crashing to earth thundered against the force of nature.

He made it to the car and dived to the ground. The tornado hit, hammering him with leaves, limbs, dirt, and bits of metal and timber. A chunk of jagged wood hit him on his left cheek, searing his skin. His face burning and wet with blood, Micah crawled to the car and managed to find enough space by one wheel to press his upper body underneath it, praying it wouldn't cave and crush him or take flight again and expose him to the storm's wrath.

Micah held to the tangled hay, grabbing chunks of dirt, grass and root, only to have something to hold onto. He prayed his siblings were safe in the small root cellar that also served as a storm shelter. They should know to stay in the small enclosed room under the stairs until the storm passed. No matter what.

He lay there with his head down, praying

that his community wouldn't be destroyed. Hoping that his brother and sister would be safe inside the house. Praying that the scream he'd heard coming from this car would show someone alive inside. He'd lost his parents three years ago in a horrible buggy accident involving a drunk driver. He did not want to open the door to this vehicle and find someone dead inside.

Dark memories whirled around him with the same force as the storm. He was the sole provider for his brother and sister now, so he hoped the hay crop and the produce garden wouldn't be completely destroyed.

Within seconds, the tornado lifted and the world went quiet. Too quiet. Micah squirmed out from underneath the damaged car and quickly stood to wipe trash, leaves and damp dirt away from one of the windows.

Then he saw her. A young woman with long blond hair lay slumped over the steering wheel, her eyes closed. He heard a shy yelping sound. The woman?

Micah checked the tiny back seat and saw

only what looked like a small suitcase and a large purse. He heard the yelping sound again and glanced at the front seat as he went around the car to check on the woman. A small black-and-white spotted dog lifted out from under a blue blanket, shivering and wide-eyed with fright.

Micah tried to open the door. Stuck. Glancing around, he hurried to the back door on the driver's side. With one jiggle, it flew open as if the entire hinge had broken loose, throwing Micah off balance. The dog yelped again and the woman lifted her head and moaned.

Micah managed to reach through and pull on the handle of the driver's door. It finally creaked open. The woman moaned again and touched a hand to her forehead. Blood seeped between her fingers.

Pulling her hand away, Micah held her head. "It's all right. You're safe."

She blinked, her eyes a deep blue that contrasted with the sky outside and did strange things to Micah's heart. Pushing that aside, he figured she might be going into shock.

"What happened?" she asked, her voice raspy.

"Tornado," he said, worry for Emmie and Jed increasing his anxiety. "Let's get you out of this car."

She tried to move then groaned before reaching her hand out. "Patch."

Micah checked her forehead. "You've got a bad bump. No patching needed."

"Patch," she said again, her voice frantic. The dog barked and jumped into her lap.

"Patch." This time she whispered with relief, her fingers digging into the little blanket that had covered the dog. "You're all right." Lifting the dog and blanket up, she held the frightened animal close.

"Is Patch your puppy?" Micah asked while he helped her out of the car. The little animal was lean and snarly and also frightened.

She looked at Micah, her expression full of fear and apprehension. "Yes," she said. "We're in trouble and we need your help."

She wobbled and fell into Micah's arms, the puppy shivering between them.

"You sure do need help," he said. "That was some storm."

Micah needed to check on Emmie and Jed so he lifted the woman up and told the puppy to hold on. "Stay right there, little fellow, and soon you'll be warm and safe."

The woman moaned again. "Not storm. Him. After me."

She wasn't making sense. Micah tried to soothe her. "You'll be all right now."

Before he could get to the house, his brother and sister came running out, calling his name. Micah nodded to them and breathed a sigh of relief when he saw that other than some missing roof shingles and a few limbs leaning against a corner, the house was intact. Limbs and small uprooted trees were scattered all over the yard, and his vegetable garden and the cornfield had both taken a hit. He'd have to check on the neighbors later. Already he could hear sirens screaming and people's shouts echoing through the woods and fields.

"Who is that?" Emmie asked with an inquisitive frown, her gaze on the woman in his arms.

"Did she fall out of the sky?" Jed chimed in.

"Her car landed in our field out back," Micah explained as they walked toward the house, mud sloshing all around their feet. The woman's long thick hair fell in golden waves across his arm. "She's hurt but okay."

They both glanced back at the deep tire marks and the car tilted into the dirt and mud. "That'll mess up part of the grazing crop," Jed said on a pragmatic note.

"The crop will be fine," Micah retorted. "I hope." He only had four cows as it went. They had plenty of grazing grass and they'd have plenty of hay to come in the fall.

"Her car got lifted by the tornado?" Jed obviously thought that was impressive even in the dire circumstances.

The skies lit up with a strike of lightning, followed by distant thunder. Would another storm follow the tornado?

Patch got squirmy and yelped.

Emmie jumped back when they reached

the long back porch, her hands fisted at her side. "What is wrong with this woman?"

Patch stuck his little head out of the tiny blanket Micah had somehow found in his arms, too. A soft, uncertain bark greeted the *kinder.*

"A dog," Emmie said, grinning with glee. "She has a puppy dog. He's so cute. He looks like he's wearing a big black smudge over one eye."

"Quiet now," Micah cautioned, wet hair plastered to his mud-caked face. "Let's get them both inside. She might need a doctor and I need to check on the animals."

"Can I hold the dog?" Emmie asked, her motherly nature kicking in as she eyed the squirming dog.

"*Ja,* but be careful," Micah said as he allowed her to grab the blanket and Patch. "Let's get Patch's friend settled and we'll feed little Patch."

Emmie giggled and cooed. "Patch, you are so cute." She carefully wrapped the little yelper back into the blanket, swaddling him like a *bobbeli*. The dog looked up at her with grateful, soulful eyes.

Micah thought he heard footsteps coming around the side of the house. When he glanced over that way, no one appeared. Voices echoed in the wind. Maybe the neighbors were out checking on people and livestock or some of the teens on *rumspringa*, trying to make mischief. He'd have to do his own survey to see how bad the damage was. Not what he needed right now, but he was thankful that they were all alive. Including the petite *Englisch* woman in his arms.

When he heard hammering footsteps again, he whirled with the woman still in his arms. Had someone else been caught on the road that ran beside their house? The valley seemed to go silent again, making him think he was imagining more bad weather. Maybe tin bumping the house or one of the restless animals in the barn kicking. A lot of echoes hovered out over the yard. The quick storm had left things unsettled and changed.

He looked down at the woman who lay unconscious in his arms. She seemed frightened of more than just the storm. Where had she been headed?

Or more to the point, where had she come from? And what was she running from?

TWO

Samantha grabbed at the warm blanket
covering her, her damp jeans and cotton
shirt sticking to her skin. Her heart pounded
and she had a tremendous thirst. When
she tried to sit up, dizziness overcame her.
Touching her hand to her head, she felt a
piece of gauze covered with two strips of
bandages.

Where was she?

Blinking, she lay still until her injured
head stopped spinning. Taking a tentative
glance around, she took in the muted lamp-
light and plain furniture. She was in someone's house. An Amish home. How had she
gotten here?

Her head buzzed and hummed and finally settled. The car. The storm. Wind and
darkness. A truck ramming her car over

and over. The truck she'd feared seeing had been chasing her. A tornado!

This wasn't Gramma's house. Who had found her? She strained to see out the window. Darkness had settled into shadows, making her think someone was out there waiting to harm her. Would *he* make them bring her back?

"Patch?" she called, her words barely above a whisper. "Patch?" she cried, her voice rising. She had to get her dog and get out of here, but where could she go now?

Why had she thought this would be a good idea, to hide in her grandmother's empty house?

The door opened and a man walked in. An Amish man.

Samantha stared up at him, the light from a nearby lamp shining on his jawline and eyes. Dark eyes and dark curly hair clung to his forehead and curved against his neck. He didn't have a beard, so he must be single.

"I remember you," she said, pushing up on the pillow to get a closer look at him. He'd rescued her. She'd only caught a glimpse of his face before she'd passed out. His voice had been deep, calm and sure. She noticed the bandage on his left cheek. "Your face was bleeding."

"So was your head," he replied, a soft smile on his lips. "You had a bump on your forehead. We cleaned it up and put a bandage over it."

Samantha touched the bandage again and winced as she felt the tender spot. "Thank you." She looked at the gauze on his cheek. "Are you all right?"

"Nothing I can't handle," he said. "Do you hurt anywhere besides your head?"

She moved around, her muscles protesting. "I'm good, other than being scared out of my wits." And not just because of the tornado. She'd almost let it slip about the truck trying to run her off the road. "The wind lifted my car and I remember screaming. Then a jolt and pain. I must have hit the roof of the car."

"That was a mean one," he said. "Brought down a lot of trees. I saw your car ramming into the hay field. I got caught in the storm and had to slide against the car and wedge myself under it and wait the storm out." He explained how he'd found her and Patch.

"I'm sorry you had to do that," she replied, horrified that he could have been hurt trying to help her. She wanted to ask if he'd seen the truck but decided against that. She squinted, her head throbbing. "Did I hear children?"

"My brother and sister," he explained. "They're with Patch right now. He's a feisty little thing."

Breathing a sigh of relief, she asked, "Is everything okay with your property?" Surely he'd mention the truck if he'd seen it. She had a vision of the truck being pushed by the tornado's force.

Murky memories floated to the surface. The truck had flipped into the ditch at the edge of his property. She could have dreamed the truck was chasing her, but she believed this nightmare was real. She'd never told anyone in Winter Lake that she used to be Amish so how had they found her so quickly?

The man watching her now nodded. "I made sure the barn was still together and tried to settle the animals. I wanted to talk to you before I go out again to clean up limbs and check for leaks in the barn and on the roof."

Panic slushed through her with the same stickiness her clothes held. Now, a fear greater than her pain filled her with a deep dread. What if those people who'd been tailing her were still out there? They could have survived and could now be looking for her on foot.

"How long have I been here?" she asked. She could sneak away again after dark, but without her car that would be hard to accomplish.

"About an hour," he replied, studying her with a quietness that put her on edge. His suspicion was obvious. He would have questions that she didn't want to answer.

She looked him over now that he was closer and she wasn't seeing two of him. His hair curled in a rebellious way even after he raked a hand through it. His eyes were dark but held a hazel tint of gold as they widened with an unyielding interest. He had a strong face, a face that looked honed by hard work, yet still remained handsome. His frown seemed permanently etched. Or maybe he frowned at having her here.

Samantha felt the same interest she saw in his eyes. He was a stranger who'd been forced to help her. "What's your name?" she asked to calm herself.

"I'm Micah King," he said. "I live here with my younger twin siblings Emma, or Emmie as we call her, and Jed, or Jedidiah as he hates to be called."

That made her smile. "He has a long name like me. I'm Samantha Herndon. Or Samantha as I like to be called."

"*Gut* to meet you, Samantha," he said. "Other than going through a tornado, I mean."

She wanted to ask why he didn't have a wife and why he lived with his siblings. Who else stayed in this house?

That made her apprehension skyrocket again. None of that mattered. She had to keep moving and she needed to be very careful about what she revealed to him.

"Patch?" she asked, barely able to breathe when she thought about her little dog. Her car had to be ruined and…people were searching for her. She had an intriguing man standing in front of her. Right now, she was worried about the dog that had started all of this.

Micah put a hand on her arm. "Patch is being pampered and spoiled by Emmie and Jed. They made him a bed in the mudroom and we've fed him some chopped chicken. He should be fast asleep by now."

"Thank you," she said, dropping back on the pillow. "When I feel better, I'll look him over."

"Like a doctor?" he asked, surprised.

"Yes. I'm an animal doctor."

When she coughed, he went to a dresser and poured water out of a pitcher. "Here, drink this. I'll bring you some soup later."

Samantha took the water and gulped it

down, glad he hadn't pressed her on what she'd said. She wasn't ready to talk about the details of her life with him. She had to find a way out of here. She needed to get safely to her grandmother's house because she knew her grandmother was away. She could hide there without endangering Gramma.

"More?" he asked when she handed the glass back.

Shaking her head, she said, "No. Where is my car?"

"Still out in the field," he said. "I wanted to make sure you're all right before I make my rounds to check on things. I'll see how bad the damage is. I did bring in your suitcase and purse." He pointed to a tall walnut armoire against the far wall. "Inside there."

She shook her head, causing a rush of dizziness. "I can't stay."

"You're injured," he said. "Your car is damaged. I don't think you'll be able to leave right now with all the roads blocked by downed trees. I can call someone to get you to a medical facility."

"No."

The one word hung in the air between them for a moment.

"What else can I do for you?" he asked, coming back around to another suspicious study of her.

"You have to hide my car," she said, panic circulating with each beat of her pulse.

"The car?" Puzzled, Micah glanced out the window at the big sloping field. "Why?"

Fear shined in her eyes. Would she tell him the truth?

"What's going on with you, Samantha Herndon?" Staring her down, he watched the flush of emotions coloring her skin. The fear was replaced by a taut determination that he didn't trust. "Why do I need to hide your car?"

She looked up at Micah, dread filling her eyes. "I can't lie. I'm trying to get away from someone. I think they found me. A truck rammed into my car when the storm hit."

Micah's distrust changed to concern.

"You mumbled something—about *him* being after you."

"Two men in a big black truck. They tried to run me into a ditch. I think someone sent them—to follow me."

"So you're saying the truck sent your car flying?"

"They rammed the truck against my car and tried to push me off the road, then the storm hit. The wind tossed the truck and shoved it toward the ditch. It flipped and landed on its side. It's probably still out there. They'll come back even if it's on foot. I need to leave before they do that. I won't put you and your family in danger."

Glancing toward where they could hear the children laughing in the other room, he whirled around. "I heard footsteps after the storm when I was bringing you inside. Why do you need to get away? Is it your husband? A boyfriend?"

Shame poured over her with a heat that left her flushed again. Micah rushed to get her more water. Her hands shook so badly, she couldn't take the glass. "I should leave. I need to get out of here."

She tried to stand, but she stumbled and held a hand to her head, dizzy. Micah caught her with one strong arm while he set the glass of water down with the other.

After helping her lie down, he said, "I told you, you can't go out there. The roads are full of fallen trees and your car tires are partially buried in mud and debris, not to mention we don't even know if your car will crank. Besides, I can tell you're in no condition to drive."

Samantha gripped the quilt, her knuckles white. "You have to take me to Martha Byler's place. She's my *grossmammi*. I was headed to her house."

Micah's expression registered the shock jarring through him. "Martha—your *grossmammi*?"

Samantha nodded, tears in her eyes. "I… I used to be Amish. I left when I was young. I call her Gramma."

Micah saw the pain in her eyes. Right now, she probably needed her gramma's arms around her, hugging her close. She'd have to wait on that.

He sank down in the chair by the bed. "You do not know."

"What?" Samantha managed to sit back against the pillow, a questioning look in her eyes. "What? Did something happen to my grandmother?"

"No. She's fine," Micah replied. "She left for the summer. Went to see her sister in Indiana. Laura Troyer, I believe?"

"Aunt Laura." Samantha bobbed her head. "I know, but I was in a big hurry to leave New York. I'd hoped she'd be back by now."

"You drove from New York to get here?"

She nodded, weariness in her next words. "I live in upstate New York and I left late last night." She took a deep breath. "I stopped on the road and started out again this morning. The weather turned bad all across the state. I thought if I could get to Gramma's house, I'd be okay." Putting a hand to her mouth, she said, "They found me. I don't know how. I saw them."

"Who are they?"

Samantha gave him an imploring stare. "I'd rather not say."

Micah's mood darkened while he gave her another direct stare. "Who is trying to harm you? I need to know. You can't leave yet so we have to be prepared."

She tried to get up again. "I won't get you involved. Just take me to Gramma's. I know where she keeps the key and I'm familiar with her home. I'll be fine there."

Again, he stopped her with a gentle touch on her arm. "You can't go there alone and hurt. Not if someone is after you."

"I'll be okay after some food and sleep," she said even as she slipped underneath the quilt. "I'll find a way to leave once I'm feeling better."

A loud knock at the front door caused Samantha to cower underneath the covers. With a stubborn frown, she took a breath and sat back up. "You have visitors."

Micah glanced back at the partially open door and said, "We will talk later."

He rushed toward the open bedroom door, his mind reeling with more questions and unease. "Stay here," he said, glancing back. "It's probably the neighbors checking on us. You need to stay out of sight and quiet, just in case."

Samantha called out, "Micah, make sure Patch is out of sight, too."

Micah gave her a nod before he closed the door.

He wasn't sure if he could believe her or trust her. She'd fallen into a big batch of trouble and that trouble had followed her here.

THREE

While Micah checked the door, Samantha's mind went to work on how to get out of this situation, especially how she could get from here to her grandmother's house without anyone seeing her. Walking was common around here, but she'd been away for years and she was disoriented and confused.

Normally, she met problems and challenges head-on. These people were wicked and they wanted her dead. She'd taken off so fast she'd barely had time to form a plan.

If she'd only made it to her gramma's house, she could be hiding there now. Of course, the storm might have damaged the small farmhouse. Thankful that her grandmother wasn't there, she thought about her options. She could sneak out right now and make her way there.

If she left once it was full dark, maybe she'd have a better chance. She only had to follow the road a few miles. The storm had changed everything so it might be a challenge. She had her phone, but she needed to reserve the battery until she could get into town and talk to the local police or find a place to boot up her laptop and find the files she'd saved.

Patch would be able to smell the scent of whoever was looking for them. He'd bark a warning. The same kind of warning he'd barked when she'd found the dog wandering in the woods after she'd gone on a long jog. The little fellow had practically forced her to follow him back to the bad place. What she'd seen there had sent chills down her spine.

She'd taken Patch to her clinic and cleaned him and vaccinated him, her assistant Dorothea helping her. They'd worked together providing medical help for many animals, but Patch had touched both of them.

"Such a sweet little boy," Dorothea said over and over, her brown eyes full of compassion. Older than Samantha by ten years, she'd been at the Winter Lake Veterinarian Clinic since it opened. She knew the work almost as well as Samantha did and she had gone through certification training to add to her credentials. "You know, he reminds me of Clyde's little dog." Giving Samantha a confused stare, she added, "You know, Clyde, that old homeless man we see in town now and then."

Samantha couldn't tell her friend the truth so she played dumb. "I found him while I was jogging," she said. "He doesn't seem to have a chip to identify him so I have no way of verifying that."

Dorothea had checked the dog over again. "Are you going to keep him?"

"I'm planning on it for now," Samantha had replied. She didn't reveal to Dorothea what she'd seen on the long road off the beaten path. At that time, she didn't want to falsely accuse anyone, especially her fiancé. Dorothea knew Leon Stanton, but she didn't seem to like him very much.

Samantha did what she had to do. She

didn't tell anyone she planned to sneak back to that big warehouse hidden deep in the woods to get evidence of what she'd seen. She should have called the police first thing, but Samantha had to be sure of what she'd discovered. She needed to see the truth in front of her and accept that the man she loved had a life she wasn't even aware of, a life no one in the community could possibly know about. No one except the unsavory characters he must have been paying to do his dirty work for him.

She'd gone back out to his vast estate late one night and found her way on foot back to that mysterious road. After she'd taken several photos and dictated notes into her phone, she'd found a peephole in a window.

She'd seen something that made her sick at her stomach.

She'd gasped, slipped and fell. Someone had spotted her running away in the middle of the night. Samantha had made it back to her car and hurried home and gathered some clothes and her laptop. She'd called Dorothea and told her she had to go out of town for a few days to visit her grand-mother. Dorothea had assumed Gramma was sick and Samantha hadn't elaborated. No time to explain.

Because she knew they'd kill her to keep her quiet and they'd do the same to Dorothea if Samantha told her the truth.

When one of them had shown up and parked his car across from her apartment, she and Patch had managed to sneak around back and get to where she'd hidden her car.

Now she knew everything and now they'd want to keep her quiet. She had Patch, which proved she'd been there the night they killed that man. Plus, she'd taken pictures with her phone and recorded what she could to use as evidence. They wanted her dead, so she couldn't testify against them.

Still reeling from what Samantha had told him, Micah asked Jed to take Patch to the back of the house so the dog wouldn't try to get loose.

Emmie grabbed little Patch and swooped

him away, Jed right behind her as they headed to the mudroom.

"Micah?"

Micah recognized the voice at the door. "Hold on, Isaac."

He opened the door to find Isaac Witmer and his wife, Rebecca, standing there. The older couple lived a mile or so down the way.

"Kumm," he said, stepping back. "Is something wrong? Did the storm do damage at your place?"

"Damage to our buggy," Isaac said, his clothes soaked. "We barely made it out alive."

Rebecca winced. "Isaac, we are all right."

Isaac put a hand to his mouth. "I am so sorry, Micah. I'm so frightened and shaken I was not thinking straight."

Micah patted Isaac's shoulder. People were always thoughtful about his parents' horrible death. "Sit and I'll make some coffee."

"Let me," Rebecca said, immediately touching her hand to his bandaged cheek.

"I need to do something. I'm still shaking. I'm thankful we didn't get blown away. Is your wound bad, Micah?"

"It's not too deep," he said, worried about the woman hiding in the next room.

"I can see I need to get busy with food," Rebecca replied.

Micah sat with Isaac at the long kitchen table. "So you were in your buggy when the storm hit?"

"Ja." Isaac combed his fingers through his beard. "We'd left the new produce market Tobias Mast set up. You know, it's a co-op and he has booths available to rent. The weather report sent everyone scurrying. Anyway, I saw the storm coming and I had to unhitch the Percheron because he was getting out of control. Sent him trotting toward home. We tried to stay covered, but when we heard the roar we had to dive out of the buggy. We huddled in that deep ditch that runs along the curve. Seconds after we got in the ditch, the wind picked up the buggy and sent it flying." Shaking

his head, he said, "If I hadn't let the horse go, he'd be dead now, I'm sure."

"But you were able to go into the ditch?" Micah asked, thankful they were both okay, but wondering what they'd seen. This storm causing vehicles and buggies to topple only reminded him of the day he'd been told about his parents' accident. And that they had not survived.

"We were past your driveway and about midway in the curve," Rebecca said, nodding. "I might have dreamed I saw a red car ahead of us. Figured they'd pull over somewhere."

Micah had to look away. "I'm haven't made it out to check much of the property."

"Did you see that pickup truck?" Isaac asked. "A big black one. It went speeding past us as we lay there in the ditch and watched our buggy collapse like a folded napkin. Almost hit the buggy even as it went flying." Isaac shrugged. "Come to think of it, I don't know where that truck wound up either."

Micah's nerves tingled with apprehension.

"I never saw a truck. I thought I heard footsteps running in my yard. It might have been the storm still raging."

"We watched the truck disappear around the curve right behind that red car," Isaac said. "We huddled in a shallow ditch and held tight to each other. We waited until we were sure the storm was gone, then we crawled out of the ditch and hiked up here."

Isaac nodded. "*Ja*, we were worried about you. We saw some teens rummaging through some of the debris. You know John Kemp's sons, Samuel and Matthew. Always stirring up trouble."

Micah knew of the Kemp boys. They'd been aggravations since they were wee *kinder*. Maybe they were the ones snooping near his house earlier. "I'll keep an eye out," he said, thinking he had no choice.

"We're all a little rattled," Rebecca said, shaking her damp skirt.

"Let me get you some towels," Micah said. "After coffee, I'll go with you, Isaac, to see how badly your buggy is damaged."

When he opened the mudroom door, hoping to get a towel and shut the door again, the little dog bolted out of Emmie's arms and started barking at Isaac and Rebecca.

"I'm sorry, Micah," Emmie said.

"*Kumm* out and see the Witmers," Micah replied, grabbing two big clean towels. He couldn't be angry at his siblings. It wasn't their fault that a storm had dropped a beautiful woman who was on the run with a dog right into their laps.

"What have we here?" Rebecca asked, her hands on her hips before she immediately lifted the barking dog up in her arms. "Did you two get a new pup or is he lost in the storm?"

"Kind of," Jed said, glancing toward Micah.

Rebecca looked puzzled. "Kind of which one?"

Micah turned to face Rebecca. "We found a woman hurt in a car. It might be the same car you saw earlier. She's resting in the spare room down the hall. She's still frightened. I didn't want to alarm you. The dog belongs to her. I'm sorry I wasn't honest about it."

"Well, mercy," Rebecca said, handing the dog back to Emmie. "You've had a lot of excitement here." After taking the towel Micah offered, she started dabbing at her wet dress. "The woman—is she all right?"

"She's hungry," Emmie said, shrugging. "I heard her and Micah talking about soup."

Micah wondered what else Emmie and Jed had heard. He gave Isaac a towel and was about to explain more.

Tossing the damp towel she'd draped around her neck down onto a chair, Rebecca turned back toward the kitchen. "Maybe I can find her something to eat."

Micah glanced at Isaac. Isaac shrugged and smiled. Rebecca was a take-charge kind of woman and she had five sons and eight grandchildren. No one dared dispute her.

This was getting out of hand. Soon the whole community would know he had a hurt woman in his house, a hurt woman running from someone dangerous.

"Why don't I introduce you to Samantha

before you worry about preparing a meal," Micah said. "Isaac and I can go and see what can be done with your damaged buggy before it's too dark to tell."

He'd have some explaining to do to both Samantha and the Witmers. Right now, his friend needed help and Micah had a thousand concerns on his mind. He could only tackle them one at a time, so he had to start somewhere.

Samantha waited, holding her breath. She'd heard voices that sounded more friendly than dangerous, but she couldn't relax.

When a knock come on the door, her heart jumped. "Yes?"

Micah leaned around the door. "I have to go help a friend with his buggy. His wife will stay here with you and the *kinder*. Do you mind that?"

What should she say? She sure didn't want to be alone. She also didn't want to put anyone else in danger. Nodding her head, Samantha tried to smile. "That's fine."

Before Micah could say another word, the door swung open and a plump, petite woman in water-spotted clothes stood there with a big smile on her face.

Micah lifted his shoulders in an awkward shrug. "Samantha, this is Rebecca Witmer. She's going to make you something to eat."

"Hello," Samantha said, wondering what she should say to the woman. *Hi, some dangerous people are looking for me, so run for your life.*

Before she could form a thought, Rebecca waved Micah away. "Go help Isaac. I've got this handled."

After Micah hurried out, Rebecca came over to the bed and touched a hand to the bandage on Samantha's head. "Micah told us what happened. I know you're frightened and maybe we Amish make you uncomfortable. Micah is a *gut* man. He's been through a lot. His *daed* and *mamm* were the kindest people. Tragic what happened to them."

"What?" Samantha grabbed the quick silence to speak. "What did happen to them?"

"A buggy accident," Rebecca said in a

whisper before stepping back. "A drunk driver hit them from behind. They were both killed."

"Oh." Samantha couldn't stop her gasp or the shock that ran through her. She'd assumed he had a girlfriend somewhere or maybe parents. To lose his folks that way was unimaginable. No surprise now why he'd frowned as she'd described what happened to her. Putting that aside, she asked, "He's raising his brother and sister by himself?"

"*Ja*, and doing a fine job," Rebecca replied, her praise genuine. "Got all kinds of young women vying for his attention and he ignores them. Those *kinder* come first with Micah. Now, you rest and I'll go and see about some dinner. Everyone's hungry around here so I'm sure I can put together some sandwiches."

"I think that would do the trick." In spite of her anxieties, Samantha felt at ease with Rebecca. "Thank you," she said. After hearing about Micah's situation, she felt she owed Rebecca a little bit of an explanation. "And, Rebecca, I used to be Amish so I'm not uncomfortable being here. I can't stay so I'm concerned about my car...and... well...life."

That statement brought Rebecca back around. "Where are you from?"

She had to be careful. "New York."

The older woman didn't look convinced. "Who do you know here?"

"Martha Byler."

A shrewd frown. "And how do you know of Martha?"

Samantha couldn't lie. "She is my grandmother."

Rebecca slapped her hand against her leg. "Dear, sweet Martha? This is a surprise. Martha talks about her grandchildren a lot. She misses them dearly since they live in Ohio. I don't recall your name coming up." She gave Samantha a motherly glare. "Did you fall out of favor?"

"No," Samantha assured her. "Gramma calls me by my first name—Leah." Her life was one long, chaotic story, so she'd started going by her middle name, a rebellious decision that distanced her from her past. "I left by my own choice to help out my mother. I don't know my uncle very well. He has two sons and a daughter." She paused, thinking of all she'd missed. "I didn't go through *rumspringa* or get baptized. I haven't been Amish for a long time. I keep up with Gramma through letters and I always respect her faith and way of life."

Rebecca clapped her hands together. "So you're little Leah?"

"That's me," Samantha replied. "You probably don't remember me."

"I remember the name since Martha does mention you a lot. She seems sad sometimes when she speaks of you." Rebecca studied her in the same way Micah had. "Did you come to see her then? I know she'd love a visit as long as it's proper and follows our rules."

Samantha didn't push on that subject. She knew she would be accepted by her grandmother because she had been accepted in Gramma's home when no one else wanted Samantha. "I was on my way to her house when the storm hit. Micah says she is away for the summer." It wouldn't help to tell Rebecca she'd come here to hide *while* her grandmother was away.

"*Ja*, and she'll be distressed that she missed you. Her older sister, Laura, is not well so she felt it necessary to go and take care of her."

"I so wanted to see her," Samantha admitted. "Sometimes, you just need your *grossmammi*'s hug. I miss her so much."

Rebecca's skeptical expression softened. "How about I give you a hug in her place and one day, you can hug someone else for me?"

Tears sprang to Samantha's eyes. "I'd like that."

Rebecca came to the bed and tugged Samantha into her arms. "Some sandwiches, and maybe pie?"

Samantha could only nod. Rebecca smelled of lemon wax and goat's milk lotion—just as her gramma used to. An ache hit Samantha in her heart. "I shouldn't have come here."

"Nonsense," Rebecca said. "*Gott* brings everyone home sooner or later, in His own way."

When they heard a crash outside, they parted.

"I wonder what that was?" Rebecca stood and went toward the window. Darkness from the storm and the dusk had cast everything into hulking shadows. The wind whipped in gusts and wails. "Maybe the storm damaged the roof and something fell off in the wind."

Samantha hoped Rebecca was right, but instincts told her they were in trouble. She sat up, waiting for the dizziness to hit her. Her head didn't spin. She shook, whether from hunger or fear, or both. Her head pounded in protest like a hundred woodpeckers chipping away at her brain each time she tried to move. Her limbs shivered with a numbness that left her weak. Wishing Micah would hurry back, Samantha managed to hold onto one of the headboard spindles.

Emmie came running in, Patch and Jed

behind her. "There's a big man walking around our yard, Rebecca. *Englisch*—and he has a gun."

FOUR

Micah and Isaac had taken flashlights with them since the skies grew darker with each minute. They walked the half mile quickly, misty rain clinging to their shirts and pants.

Sirens whistled from the town center, making Micah think the storm had done a lot of damage somewhere. His place was a mess but intact, at least. Thankful for that, he remembered how his neighbors had helped him build a new barn over a year ago. One that had survived this storm, thankfully.

"I see people are out and about," Isaac said as they came to the road. "I hope no one was hurt."

"Or worse," Micah added, since he knew they were both thinking that. Funny, how careful people were around someone who'd lost loved ones. He loved talking about his parents and tried to do so often with the twins. It made the twins feel better and it sure helped him, too. It sometimes made others feel awkward. They didn't know what to say and what could they say besides the same old platitudes? *Gott*'s will was sometimes hard to follow, but the tenets of his faith demanded it.

The Amish accepted this. Still, the pain of loss was sometimes a palpable thing that chased at his dreams.

Putting his mind back on the task at hand, Micah let out a sigh and surveyed the countryside. He couldn't find the truck Samantha had described. From what Isaac had said, the truck should be near the eastern side of his driveway. Isaac's buggy was on the western side, so he'd been behind Samantha's car and the truck following her. Someone had to have spotted it by now.

Had the two men escaped unharmed or were they injured and taken away for treatment?

Fire trucks and ambulances came and

went and cars passed, the people inside looking left and right at the vast swath the storm had taken across the fields and valleys. When they spotted their friend Jeremiah Weaver on the volunteer fire truck, they waved. Usually an Amish volunteer rode a horse or a motorized scooter to the fire. With this storm, Jeremiah had probably gone to work helping where he could and had waited for the truck to show up so he could hop on.

Micah had known Jeremiah a few years now. He'd come home after being away for twelve years and married his sweetheart Ava Jane, who had become a widow while he was away. They were happy now. Jeremiah, however, had retained some of the *Englisch* ways—volunteering to fight fires and, after saving Ava Jane's daughter from drowning in the deep part of the creek, teaching all the area *kinder* how to swim. Micah wished he could find someone like Ava Jane. He'd had lots of the local Amish women vying for his time. Nothing ever came of it. He hadn't found the one yet.

Samantha came into his head. He had to admit, she was pretty and she seemed smart. She was *Englisch,* though, and right now she was scared and holding her secrets close. He couldn't have trouble coming to his house. He had to protect Emmie and Jed, above all else. He needed to get this done and head home.

The truck slowed and Jeremiah leaned out of the passenger's side window. "Is everything okay?"

Isaac pointed to where his buggy lay in the nearby field. "My buggy is messed up, but Rebecca and I are fine. She is up at Micah's house with…the *kinder.*"

Micah appreciated Isaac's discretion. He had a problem waiting back at home and he wasn't sure how to handle it yet.

"We can help with the buggy," Jeremiah said after turning to tell the driver to pull the pump truck off the road. "We've checked on all of our families and everyone along the road. A lot of damage and downed trees, but no one missing and no one hurt other than cuts and bruises, thankfully." Nodding to

Micah, he said, "I see you've got a bandage there. What can we do?"

Isaac looked at the darkening sky. "Help us upright the buggy and see how bad the damage is?"

Jeremiah nodded at the request, then he and the two men with him got out of the truck.

"Any automobile accidents?" Micah asked.

"A couple," Jeremiah replied. "Another buggy with a bent tire rim and a pickup truck about a quarter mile from here. Abandoned. It'll take a tow truck to pull that thing out of the big ditch—just as you exit Green Mountain Road."

"Told you a truck passed us," Isaac said to Micah.

Micah kept his expression neutral. "No idea of who was in it?"

"Neh," Jeremiah replied. "I hope they were able to walk away. Let's have a look at your buggy, Isaac."

Micah's heart pumped fear along with adrenaline. He had to get back to his house. Those two men could have been on his property when he went out to Samantha's car and brought her inside. He didn't want to think about what might have happened if he hadn't helped her. He couldn't get the sound of those stomping footsteps he'd heard out of his head.

He couldn't leave Isaac and the others without offering help either. When two horses came trotting up, he recognized Samuel and Matthew Kemp. They hopped off their horses and hurried up.

"We can help," Samuel said, his expression more of a smirk than a smile.

"Then *kumm*," Isaac said, giving Micah a concerned glance. "We need all the help we can get."

Matthew and Samuel marched along with them, asking questions as they went. Did they see the storm? Had they heard a truck was in the ditch?

Inquisitive and impulsive, Micah thought. Were they here to help or make trouble? They were mostly known for that.

As the men slushed through the field toward the buggy, Micah stared off in the distance. Isaac noticed his distraction. "Are you worried about something, Micah?"

"I don't know how to deal with having an *Englisch* woman in my home," he admitted on a low voice. "She's hurt and without transportation."

Isaac watched him carefully. "Do what you can for her and tomorrow, you can give Samantha a ride to a doctor. Or we can send Jeremiah and the paramedics up to check on her."

"I think she's fine. Her wounds are not serious, but she did take a good bump on her head. I'll check on her again when we get back."

"Might be smart to be aware," Isaac replied, glancing ahead. "A lot of people out and about with this storm. We spotted these Kemp boys earlier riding their horses and shouting like hooligans. Didn't bother to stop and help anyone. Have to keep an eye on 'em."

The boys kept asking Jeremiah and the others all about the tornado, then went on to explain how they'd seen a truck flying off the road. The same truck that had been chasing Samantha?

Micah got a weird feeling in his stomach. He needed to get back to his house. How could he be sure his family was safe?

Jeremiah and Isaac were already tugging on the ruined open buggy while the other two volunteers checked the axle. The axle was bent and one of the tire rims lay twisted in an awkward angle. Micah glanced back at the road and then back to Isaac.

"We can move it to the road," Jeremiah offered, his strong arms showing he could probably move anything.

All the men found a place to hold on to and with a grunt, Jeremiah gave the nod. They lifted the heavy buggy and slowly trudged through the wet field.

Finally, out of breath, Isaac said, "Stop. Leave it here."

They were not far from the road. Micah's fears were growing as the darkness settled over them.

"I'll get some people together first thing

tomorrow," Isaac said. "It's too damaged and it's getting dark." Glancing around, he shook his head. "I worry about looters and curious *Englisch.*"

Micah nodded. "It might be best to leave the buggy for now. I need to check on Emmie and Jed. Rebecca has been with them a while."

They all walked back to the road and Jeremiah and the others got in the fire truck. The boys got on their horses and took off.

Micah waved to Jeremiah. "Could you give us a ride back to my place?"

"For sure," Jeremiah said. "Hop on the back."

Isaac thanked them with a shout and turned back to Micah after they grabbed hold on the back fender and hopped up to grab onto the rig. "Are you concerned about your visitor?"

Isaac could always read people. Probably why he was now one of the district ministers.

"Well, she did show up during a storm and

she is *Englisch*," Micah replied. "I haven't decided if I trust her or not."

"You were hiding her, ain't so?"

He wouldn't lie to Isaac. The man had been the first person to show up when Micah had learned of his parents' deaths.

"Ja."

Isaac watched the rig lights dancing in front of the grinding truck. "Were you concerned about improprieties or something more?"

"Both," Micah admitted.

As they approached the end of the gravel drive up to Micah's house, they both hopped down and waved thanks to Jeremiah and the others. The big fire truck pulled away.

Isaac asked, "What something more?"

Micah was about to tell him when they heard a scream, followed by Patch's frantic barks, coming from the house. Micah took off at a run and heard Isaac's footsteps doing the same behind him.

His instincts had been correct. A hulking shadow moved along the side porch of his house.

* * *

Footsteps dragged with a heavy beat across the porch.

The minute Samantha had heard Jed's alert, she'd motioned to Rebecca. "We need to lock all the doors."

Rebecca had given her a puzzled glimpse and started to the back, but stopped to pick up the glass water pitcher on the table next to the bed. "Just in case," she'd whispered. "This will make a *gut* weapon."

Samantha had managed to move with her despite her dizziness. "I'll go to the front. Meet me back in the hallway." She motioned to the children. "Is the mudroom door locked?"

Jed had nodded. "I locked it when I first saw the man coming from the field. He was headed toward the house."

Samantha's apprehension had now doubled as adrenaline rushed through her system. Whoever was out there had probably searched her car. Micah had put her purse and laptop and a few clothes in the armoire in the bedroom. Her phone was there, too.

She'd turned off notifications and the location app. Had that been enough? What if he'd come to take her laptop? She had important evidence hidden in her private files. Photos she'd managed to snap before they'd spotted her. She couldn't let whoever that was inside this house.

"Come with me," Rebecca said to the children. "Jed, go with Samantha to secure the front of the house. Emmie and I will check the back."

"We need a plan," Jed said in a voice that sounded firm. He didn't move.

"If he comes in the back, we run out the front," Samantha said to the children. "Understand?"

"Or if he comes in the front, we head out back," Rebecca added, motioning him to follow. "If all else fails, we try to hide and stay calm until the men return."

Satisfied, Jed went with Samantha, a shaking Patch in his arms. "Will Patch protect us?" he asked.

Samantha hoped the little dog wouldn't

bark. She couldn't stop him if he did. "He'd fight to protect us, *ja?*"

"We heard someone on the porch," Rebecca said, terror in her voice as she rushed to the front with Emmie. "Must be a looter. Why would anyone be so mean?"

"I'm glad we thought to lock all the doors," Emmie replied in a whisper. "I want Micah to come home."

Jed put his arm around her. "It will be all right."

Touched by that gesture, Samantha held her breath as they all huddled near the front door. This was all her fault. She needed to keep moving. As soon as Micah returned, she'd ask him to take her somewhere. Maybe to the authorities, if she could trust them. The man she'd left had connections.

She would not put anyone here in danger. She should have known better than to come here in the first place. She'd lived here with her grandmother when she was very young. Her mother had remarried and got her life back together and they'd moved away. Samantha had felt safe with Gramma.

Now she didn't feel safe anywhere.

Coming back to the present, she kept Patch close since the little ball of fur sensed something was wrong. The poor fellow had been frightened of the storm and all of this confusion.

Listening as someone tried to open the back door, they all huddled against the corner by the front door. Samantha tried to calm herself by studying the layout of the house. A big living area and kitchen, braided rugs covering linoleum floors. A long central hallway that gave them a full view of the back door. The mudroom back there served as a bathroom, too. It must be near the room she'd been in. A staircase off the living room that apparently led to more bedrooms upstairs.

Should they take the stairs and hide there? Or would that force them into a corner? Maybe they could sneak out to the roof. Then what?

A hard hit on the wooden door down the hallway made the whole house shake.

"He's coming," Emmie said, shuddering

against Samantha's arm around her. "He must be on the side porch. We could hide in the root cellar."

Patch did a low growl, then started barking—an aggressive, protective bark that warned Samantha of someone dangerous. Someone the little dog recognized. Patch's nose lifted as he sniffed the air.

Did he smell the danger?

"We could go down in the cellar," she said. "Is there a way out of there?"

Jed shook his head and listened at the front window. "I think someone is coming this way, too. I see figures out near the road. The cellar might be the only place to hide."

"Not another one," Rebecca said, her voice shaky, but her expression stern. "I will use this glass pitcher on his head."

"We aren't to be violent," Emmie warned.

"We have to protect family," Jed replied, scooting to where a knitting basket sat. He lifted out a long needle. "I'll stab him with this."

Emmie didn't argue with that. "Patch can bite him."

Samantha prayed a fast, scattered prayer, remembering how Gramma had said when you're in a hurry, pray, *Help me, Lord.* She didn't want these innocent children and sweet, kind Rebecca to be in any danger.

Straightening a bit, she said, "You three take Patch and go into the cellar. I can go out there and talk to the man. He's probably looking for me."

Rebecca gave her a measured stare but didn't question why she would say that. "You will do no such thing," she said. "You are a guest in Micah's house so we will make sure you are safe. Somehow." She looked directly at Samantha. "I don't think the cellar is a good idea."

The door rattled again. Patch's barks became loud and choppy, angry with a pent-up rage. Her little protector was a fierce survivor. Well, so was she.

"We'll do what we planned," Samantha said, motioning for them to stand. "Let's run out front. I'll scream as loudly as I can. People are out everywhere because of the storm. Surely someone will hear us if we all shout and scream."

"*Ja*, and that bad man will run away," Jed said with a solemn surety. "Patch will scare him."

The noise at the back door increased. Thankful that the Amish built strong houses, Samantha stood and guided the children between herself and Rebecca. Handing Patch to Jed, she said, "Hold on to him. Don't let him go unless you have no other choice."

Jed nodded, his dark eyes so like his brother's and his hair a curly mess, same as Micah's. "Emmie will help."

Emmie nodded, her eyes wide with trepidation.

"Okay, if anything goes wrong," Samantha said, "head toward the road and take Patch with you."

Rebecca inclined her chin in agreement and with a show of support. "You hear? You run to the road and find help."

Samantha hoped she'd made the right decision. If she could get them all away from the house, she'd try to backtrack and distract their intruder.

Somehow.

Slowly, she opened the front door. "Run as fast as you can," she reminded the children. "Jed, keep your sister close."

Jed glanced at Emmie. "I will. Emmie, you can run as fast as me, remember. So we'll race to the road."

"I can do that," Emmie replied, taking up the challenge.

Rebecca didn't look so sure. "Keep going," she said to Samantha under her breath. "I don't want to slow anyone down with my bad knee. One reason I didn't want to go in the cellar. You three could."

"I'll give you a head start," Samantha told her. "I'll follow so we can stick together."

Rebecca nodded and looked back. "Don't wait too long."

Samantha held to the front door, her head swirling. Taking a deep breath, she watched as Rebecca raced toward the twins.

The man at the other door pushed harder.

She heard the thump of what could only be a silenced bullet. He'd shot out the lock.

"Keep going," she called, fear making her heart rate bump too high. "I'm right behind."

Samantha saw the twins and Rebecca hurrying away. Rebecca glanced back once. Then the back door burst open and Samantha turned and came face-to-face with a man she recognized as one of Leon's security guards.

She froze, shock and dread clawing at her while she stood in the open doorway to the front. Maybe she could stall him long enough for the others to get away. "What do you want?"

The man advanced, his beefy fingers twitching as he aimed the gun. "He wants you to come home. You have to come with me."

Samantha had no way out. She heard voices shouting in the front yard. "Jed? Emmie?"

"Micah," Emmie said, her voice carrying through the night. "It's Micah and Isaac."

Samantha heard Rebecca screaming, "Run, run to them."

Relief washed through Samantha. Seeing the doubt on the big man's face, she said, "You need to leave before they find you."

The man advanced, waving the gun. "I have to bring you back."

Samantha screamed with all of her might, startling the man. Without thinking it through, she whirled around through the open front door and tried to run, still screaming.

The man came after her, grabbing one of her feet and knocking her down. Her tennis shoe fell away as she clawed the wood to get up. Her breath stopped and she gasped until she could breathe again.

She expected a bullet in her back. Instead he grabbed at her. "He wants you alive, so don't be stupid."

"I'm not going!" she shouted while she tried to see who else was out there.

Two men hurried toward the house.

Two Amish men.

FIVE

Micah looked beyond the twins and Rebecca when he heard the screams. "Where's Samantha?"

"She was supposed to *kumm* behind me," Rebecca said on a shaky voice. "A man was trying to get into the house."

"Are you all right?" Micah asked the twins as he started moving toward the house.

"They're fine. Go," Rebecca said, the words a shout.

Micah saw the pitchfork he'd used earlier to rake up debris. Grabbing it, he ran toward the house and shouted, "Stop. Let her go." He held the pitchfork like a weapon. "I have a good aim," he said, raising the pitchfork as he prepared to throw it at the man.

The man tugging Samantha stopped in

his tracks and pushed her away, then turned and ran out the open back door.

Micah rushed up the steps, thinking they could have all been killed.

After dropping the pitchfork, he lifted Samantha off the floor and held her by her arms. "Are you all right?"

She nodded, her face pale in the scant light. "He sent someone to take me. They want me alive, Micah. He's trying to get me to come back there."

Confusion warred with shock in Micah's brain. Taking her hand, he turned toward Rebecca and Isaac. "She's okay. Everyone accounted for?"

"We're all fine," Rebecca said as she stood with her husband. "Samantha, you did a brave thing standing between that intruder and the *kinder*. Are you all right?"

Samantha nodded. "Just a bit shaken."

Micah turned from the twins to face Samantha. "Did you recognize him?"

"I think I remember him," she admitted, her voice raspy and low. Giving the twins a quick glance, she said, "I'll explain later."

"He had a gun, Micah," Emmie offered as she ran up, her eyes startled with fear. "I saw him. A big *Englisch* man."

"I'm going to check on the barn," Micah said, frustration coloring his words while he stared at Samantha.

"Be careful," she warned, giving Micah what she hoped was a meaningful glance. "He might still be around."

"I'll come," Jed offered, hurrying toward the back door.

"Neh." Micah held up a hand. "You and your sister need to eat and go to bed. It's been a trying day."

Looking disappointed, Jed shrugged and hung his head.

Emmie asked, "Can Patch stay in my room?"

Micah glanced at Samantha. "I don't think that would be wise."

Rebecca stepped up. "I'll get them fed and settled, Micah. Maybe Patch can bring Emmie some comfort?"

Samantha cleared her throat. "I don't mind if it's okay with Micah."

"The dog has to sleep on the floor," he said, his gaze moving over Samantha again. What had she brought into his home? What kind of evil was chasing her?

"I'll make him a bed," Emmie replied as she ran upstairs. "C'mon, Patch. You can see my room."

Patch woofed an eager response.

Isaac remained silent as the men started toward the back door. Micah stopped to examine the wood, a frown marring his face. He gave Samantha one last glance, then hurried down the steps and out into the yard.

He'd talk to her later and he'd get the truth. This had gone from surviving a storm to trying to keep his family—and a stranger— safe from harm.

Samantha moved to the kitchen, forgetting she still wore the dirty clothes from before. Now she wished for a warm shower and her sweatpants. She washed her hands and helped Rebecca finish the sandwiches she'd started earlier.

She'd never felt so weary. First, discovering Patch a couple of days ago and then, sneaking back in the dead of night to investigate, only to see a horror happening right before her eyes. She'd been spotted by one of Leon's minions.

And now, being here in a stranger's home. A kind stranger who was concerned about his family, with friends who were now involved in her problems.

What if something happened to Micah and Isaac?

"I should go and check on them," she said, whirling so fast her dizziness returned.

Rebecca took her hand. "*Neh.* The men know what they're doing. They will be careful."

"I can't take it if something happens to any of you," Samantha replied.

"We live by God's will, Samantha," Rebecca said, her eyes kind and full of understanding. "Whatever happened to you, we won't turn away. Stay here. Don't make it worse."

Samantha went back to the task at hand,

her head throbbing with fear and guilt. Here, the memories of her grandmother telling Samantha how much she loved her seemed to rise up with the enticing scent of freshly baked bread mixed with the smell of wax candles, kerosene lamps and goat milk lotion.

Rebecca moved with quiet efficiency around the kitchen, which forced Samantha to do the same.

After what seemed like hours, the men came back in and Micah shot Samantha a firm frown before washing up at the sink.

"No one about," Isaac explained. "People like to look after a storm and some like to see what they can salvage, even if it isn't theirs to have."

Micah didn't seem convinced. "We did see footprints in a few places, but we've had a lot of people tramping around."

"What about that man?" Emmie asked as she came back down the stairs, holding Patch.

"There is no one about," Micah replied.

"He tried to harm Samantha," Emmie said, her voice quivering.

"I'm okay," Samantha told Micah's frightened sister. "I was the last one inside so he tried to scare me. Your brother stopped that."

They all sat down, the twins watching the adults with curious attention. Samantha felt the tension hanging like humidity in the room. The night was warm and muggy. She longed for a cool bath and clean clothes. She longed to turn back time. Why had she taken that path the other day?

"Say your prayers," Rebecca said, lowering her head and going silent.

Samantha did the same, respecting the Amish way of speaking to God in silence. That worked for her since she couldn't blurt out her fears and worries. She did pray that God would protect Micah and his siblings and Isaac and Rebecca.

They ate the sandwiches and fresh pickles, then had some peach cobbler that one of the single ladies had brought Micah. He barely ate his. Samantha mostly moved hers around on the dish.

Finally, after he sent Emmie and Jed upstairs and they were having coffee, he turned to Samantha. "You need to tell me exactly what's going on with you."

Isaac motioned to Rebecca. "We should get home and see to our place. Thank you for loaning us a horse and buggy, Micah."

"Don't worry about getting it back until you have yours repaired," Micah said as he stood. Giving Samantha a warning glance, he said, "I'll be right back."

"Thank you," she said to Rebecca. "For everything."

Rebecca nodded, her eyes full of a silent understanding. "Samantha, if you need a place to stay for a while, our home is open to you."

Samantha nodded, too overcome to speak.

After they'd left, Micah came back into the kitchen, his presence making the big square room shrink. "I need answers, Samantha Herndon."

Samantha pushed her cold coffee away. "I

know you do." Looking down at the beautifully worn oak table, she kept talking. "I live in a little town called Winter Lake. I have a clinic there. I've had my own practice for a couple of years after interning and later working for another doctor."

His frown relaxed, making him appear younger-looking and less concerned. "It's a good thing Patch found you."

She nodded and lowered her head. "He was bad off when I found him. Took him home so I could watch him day and night and got him cleaned up and properly vaccinated. I went back to where I found him to gather evidence."

Micah sank down on a chair. "Is that part of your job?"

"No, I had seen some things that I knew weren't legally or morally right."

She inhaled and for the first time, said it out loud. "My boyfriend, Leon Stanton, is running some sort of smuggling ring." She didn't know if she could say anything more about what she'd seen in that massive warehouse.

Micah's softened expression changed to shocked, his eyes questioning, his mouth set in a grim line. "How—"

Before she could continue, Patch barked and hurled down the stairs to run to the back door. The little dog was trembling with fear. Samantha realized Patch was trying to tell them something.

"He's warning us," she said, getting up to glance out a window. "Do you think someone's still out there?"

Micah went to the mudroom and returned with his rifle.

"No, don't do that," Samantha said. "It's not your way."

"It is if I need to protect my property and my family," he said, giving her a gentle push. "Go upstairs and tell the *kinder* I'm checking the barn again."

"Patch, come with me," she said, knowing it would be useless to argue with Micah now.

Samantha watched him go out before she ran upstairs to find the siblings huddled in the hallway. "Did you hear?" she asked.

Emmie took Patch, bobbing her head. "Is that man back?"

"I don't think so," Samantha said, willing it to be true. "The animals are still restless from the storm. It'll take them a while to settle down."

"You know a lot about animals," Jed said as they all sank down against the wall, Patch jumping from lap to lap.

"I'm an animal doctor," she replied. "That's how I found Patch."

"You saved him?" Jed asked, his eyes bright with curiosity.

"I did." More than she could ever explain to them. "He's a brave little dog. A stray lost on an old country road."

Patch's big ears lifted as he listened to the conversation with one ear and waited for Micah to return with the other one.

Samantha didn't want to think about Micah not returning. She wanted to run out there and find him, but she couldn't leave the children. Sitting here, she imagined every sound as someone stalking the property, coming back through the damaged door. The wind hissed and whined and the scant moonlight winked between ominous clouds. Shadows moved over the night.

"This has been a strange day," Emmie said, rubbing her nose. "A tornado, a cute dog and you. Now we have bad people roaming around. I miss *Daed* and *Mamm*."

There was no accusation in the girl's observations. Samantha felt a dreadful guilt anyway. What if something happened to Micah? "Rebecca told me about your parents. I'm so sorry."

Emmie's expression held a longing. "They were so wonderful *gut* to us. They are with *Gott* now." Then she quickly amended that. "Micah is the best brother. He tells us he likes the quiet, plain life."

Samantha's heart burned for these children. "You know, my *grossmammi* helped raise me. I love her so much. She likes things quiet and simple, too." They sat silent, then she said, "I guess you're not used to this much excitement."

Jed laughed. "*Neh*, the most excitement

we have is a birthing or when one of those single women brings us a cake or pie."

Samantha had to smile at that. Now she was the curious one. "So you see a lot of single women around here?"

"Too many," Jed said on a pragmatic note.

"They all want to marry Micah," Emmie said, shrugging. "He says he won't marry until he knows it's right." She put a hand to her chest. "In here—in his heart."

Samantha let that sink in, the poignancy of their brother's declaration touching her in that same spot—her heart. When she thought of how Leon had fooled her that spot shut back up and she held tight against opening it again.

"He's picky," Jed said, his lips twisted. "Or as Rebecca likes to say, his standards are too high." Shrugging, he lifted Patch up and held him close. "Micah's still mad 'cause Abby ran off with someone else."

Emmie rolled her eyes. "She didn't like Jed and me."

Samantha's heart hurt for all of them. Micah was a handsome, concerned man and these two were the sweetest preteens she'd ever met. "Well, Micah loves both of you from what I've seen," she said. "So he wants things to be good for both of you, too."

"I'm glad he's not in a hurry," Jed admitted. "Some of the women who come visiting are mean and bossy."

Emmie bobbed her head. "We heard one telling him that he should send us to live with our relatives in Indiana."

Jed giggled. "Micah showed her the door real quick. He kept the pie she brought and fed it to the hogs."

Samantha's nerves tingled even while she laughed and tried to keep the twins talking. She was getting worried. What had Micah found in the barn?

Micah made his way through the alley between the stalls, the darkness casting shadows. Every creak or twitch had him spinning on his brogans to see if anyone was lurking about. The horses and cows were safe even if they did still act jumpy and nervous. Outside, the goats seemed jittery in their corral on the back side of the barn and, farther out, the hogs grunted like they did on any given day.

Working his way along the stalls and corners, he felt the same way. His whole routine had gone off-kilter because of the tornado and because of Samantha. What was he supposed to do about her? Maybe he should have sent her home with Rebecca and Isaac. Only that would have possibly put them in danger.

When he heard a rustling near the front of the barn, he headed that way. A shadow moved. Someone took off toward the open door.

"Hey, what do you want?" he shouted, hurrying after the intruder.

Whoever it was, they kept running away.

"I will shoot you if you return," he called, his shotgun aimed into the night.

The shadow ran toward the road and disappeared.

Micah went back to Samantha's car, thinking it would take a couple of plow horses and some strong helpers to get this car out of the field. He wasn't sure it would even crank. Pulling out his pocket flashlight so he could see better, he noticed right away that someone had been in the car. Deep footprints left muddy impressions in the dirt around the vehicle. Some of them could be his, but his feet weren't as big as these shoe-prints indicated.

The dashboard compartment was open, papers spilling out, and the seats had been moved, their backs popped down. A few books and papers in the back had been shuf-fled and flung here and there.

When Micah heard what sounded like twigs breaking in the woods to the west, he understood why Patch had alerted them. Someone had been snooping and probably had stayed hidden in the woods the whole time since the tornado, waiting to get back to Samantha's car. The man who'd tried to enter the house earlier might have also gone through the car. Glad the women and Emmie and Jed had gotten away and that Samantha had fought him away for now, Micah fig-ured someone would keep coming.

She'd said the man wanted her back. Why had they searched her car? What had they been looking for and why had they risked coming back?

He checked all around and noticed a different set of footprints moving from the car to where some of the hay had been trampled all the way into the tree line, leaving a flat green path of big shoe prints. He considered shooting into the air, but that would scare the animals and the twins, and wake some of the neighbors.

All he could do now was hurry back to the house and hope no one had managed to sneak back there ahead of him. Those two men in the truck were obviously well enough to keep skulking around his land. He should have asked Jeremiah for some advice. That truck could prove the men tried to run Samantha off the road.

Deciding he had to be sure, he headed to where Jeremiah had said they'd last seen the pickup. He could vouch for Samantha if he saw the truck with his own eyes. Breathless from running, he flashed his light down into the hollowed-out ditch.

The truck was still there, banged up and lying on one side. One of the doors lay open and yawning. The men could have crawled out that way. When his light flashed on something dark on the open door, he hopped down and went closer.

The remains of what looked like a bloody handprint on the inside of the door. And more blood on both seats. The dampness had smudged the prints. The ruby-red brightness ran stark against the beige interior of the fancy truck.

These men were hurt yet they'd still managed to trespass on into the woods. They might hide out there until someone picked them up. They could have easily sneaked into the field to search the car.

Or it could have been the Kemp boys looking for money or anything else to entertain themselves. Their father had died when they were preteens and their *mamm* had a hard time controlling the two wayward teens.

Micah hurried back along the road. He could go to the phone booth and call for help, but that was a half mile down the road and people would see him and wonder what was wrong, or offer help. He wasn't ready to explain all of this yet.

Glancing back at his house, he decided he couldn't take that chance. He wouldn't leave the twins and Samantha alone and unprotected. After he got the twins settled again, Micah planned to hear the rest of Samantha Herndon's story. Because he had a dreadful feeling that there was so much more to her ordeal than she'd been able to tell him, and he needed to hear it all before he decided what he could do to help her.

Or get her away from his family.

SIX

Samantha heard the door open and hopped up to run downstairs. "Stay here with Patch," she told the twins.

They scooted to the top of the stairs, Patch between them as they watched her almost collide with Micah.

"Are you all okay?" he asked, looking from her to the twins.

"We're fine. What about you? Did you see anyone?"

Glancing at the twins, he said, "I'll be back so we can talk."

He headed up the stairs. "Let's get you both back to your rooms."

"Did that man return?" Emmie asked, a thread of fear in her words. "Are you and Samantha going to have an adult discussion?"

"The man wasn't out there." Micah gave Samantha a fleeting glance over his shoulder. "I didn't find anyone and the animals are safe." Then, "*Ja*, we are going to have an adult discussion. While you two go to sleep."

Jed didn't seem convinced. Samantha heard his voice echoing down the stairs while he held Patch close. "Patch is a *gut* watchdog, ain't so? I think he heard someone."

Micah didn't argue with his brother. "Patch is smart to be so small."

Emmie asked, "Are you going to send Samantha away like you do all the other women?"

Micah didn't answer that question, but Samantha knew the answer already. He'd want her out of his home.

The voices drifted off so Samantha went to the kitchen and found the tea tin, Micah's steel-etched look from before still on her mind. She took the heavy kettle and drew water from the kitchen sink, then turned to heat it on the propane-fueled stove. Funny, how such everyday tasks returned to her now that she was back in Campton Creek. This house was a little more modernized than Gramma's. It still remained simplistic and stark in its plainness, however.

While she waited for the water to boil, she placed tea bags in two mugs and wondered what she should do now. Micah would want the whole story and that could make things even more dangerous for him and the twins. Once she told him, she'd need to leave. Immediately.

She would have to find a way to get out of here and keep moving. She needed to get in touch with Dorothea soon. Her assistant would be worried. Maybe over the weekend, Dorothea could come and get her and they'd work up a plan on how to handle her practice. The authorities would want to question Samantha since everyone in town knew she dated Leon.

That brought another realization. How could she keep her practice open now? Leon had taken over her mortgage—a Christmas gift to her, he'd explained when she'd protested. That meant he owned the building she leased. He would destroy her if she tried to go back to Winter Lake. She had to make sure he was arrested and put away. She might have to start all over again somewhere else.

When the kettle started whistling she went back to the stove and turned off the heat. She turned back to the window. Something outside caught her eye.

A flash of light up on the road.

Was someone still out there, watching this house? Waiting until they all went to bed? She hadn't had a chance to check her purse or her overnight bag. She didn't think anyone would have come near her car in the light of day.

Micah had been thoughtful in bringing her things inside. He had no way of knowing she'd been gathering evidence before she'd had to flee.

She studied the darkness and decided she'd imagined seeing that yellowish orb floating in the night. Neighbors could still be out searching for animals or family.

"What are you doing?"

Samantha whirled so fast, she almost knocked one of the mugs off the counter. "Oh, you startled me."

Micah moved closer. "Did you see someone out there again?"

The weariness in his question hit her in her stomach. "No. I mean I was staring out the window, wondering how I can find a way to leave. I won't continue to put you and the twins in danger."

"Too late for that," he said, eying the tea with a grimace. "Someone was lurking in the barn, but he ran away. And I don't drink hot tea."

Shock caused Samantha to stop and stare at him. "I could make fresh coffee." Her suggestion echoed through the taut silence. "I'm sorry. I'm relieved you weren't hurt, going out there alone. Would you like something to eat? Some lemonade?"

"*Neh*. I want you to sit down and tell me everything. And I mean everything. Then, together we will come up with a plan because I'm in this now. These people have come onto my property at least three times in one night, if I count the footsteps I heard right after the storm."

Samantha took her chamomile tea and sank down on a chair. "I didn't have any idea that Leon was so corrupt and so cruel. If I hadn't found Patch lost and wandering along the road where I usually get some exercise, I would have found out much too late."

Micah's head came up. "Too late?"

She nodded, holding her mug close, the warmth giving her courage. "Leon had proposed to me. We'd planned to get married later this year."

Micah's dark eyes gleamed with doubt. "You were going to marry this man and you had no idea he was running an illegal smuggling operation?"

She sipped her tea and lowered her head, remembering how she'd taken off the huge diamond solitaire he'd given her on Valentine's Day and left it on her dresser. "Not a clue. I worked all day with animals, some of which he brought me. I thought he was so sweet, always rescuing strays. Thought he had a big heart. But I was wrong. He used that to get to know me, to make me think he was a fine, upstanding citizen. He is cruel and uncaring and… I get shivers thinking about being his wife."

Micah's harsh stare softened. "So you truly did not know he was operating illegal smuggling?"

"No." She sipped at her tea. "I work long hours and we mostly saw each other for dinner on the weekends. Sometimes we'd drive to the city and see a play. He never wanted to talk much about work. Everyone knew he'd inherited a big sum of money and he was good at investments—he talked about tech stocks and he always had some new-fangled technical gadget to try out. That's about all he'd told me when we first started dating and even after. I respected his need for privacy. Until the day I went down the wrong road."

Staring down into her tea, she said, "I was new in town and naive. He somehow managed to sweep me off my feet and he tried to mold me into someone I could never become."

"Now you believe he's making money smuggling? What sort of things?"

Samantha kept reliving what she'd witnessed. "Jewelry, fake designer purses, what looked like electronic equipment and... guns, rows and rows of guns of all kinds. Weapons, Micah. He's dealing in selling illegal weapons."

"How did he find out you knew?"

Samantha took a deep breath. "I jogged a lot on his property and he always cautioned me to stay on the main road since he had security there. One day I ran longer than I'd planned and came up to a gravel road. I'd never seen it before so I walked along there to cool down before I turned back. That's when I found Patch wandering around. He was terrified so I offered him a granola bar I had in my pocket." Twisting the tea bag's paper label, she shook her head. "Patch kept barking and acting as though I should follow him. So I did. That's when I stumbled on a huge building that looked like a place where someone might store heavy equipment."

"Did anyone see you?"

"Not that day. There wasn't anyone around so I peeked in a window. Most of the windows were covered in dark blinds. I saw a sliver of light in one. Then I saw the rows and rows of all kinds of stuff. When I saw the guns and electronics, I panicked and grabbed Patch and got away.

"I almost went to Leon to ask him about that warehouse, but I got busy examining Patch and nurturing him. I sneaked back in the middle of the night and climbed up on an air-conditioner unit to peek in a window."

"What? You could have fallen or worse, been shot."

She stopped, gasped. "It wasn't me they shot, Micah." Closing her eyes, she gripped the end of her T-shirt. "They shot a man I know who lived in Winter Lake. Clyde was a homeless man who took on odd jobs. A sweet man, an Army veteran who'd suffered severe wounds. I heard them talking to him, then I saw them. They had him in a chair, interrogating him. I took pictures with my phone."

"They? How many?"

"Three bodyguards and Leon," she said on a low whisper. "Leon kept hitting him and then... Leon turned to one of the men and told him to take care of it."

Micah's expression showed shock and anger. "They killed this man?"

She nodded, unable to speak.

"And you saw this happen?"

"Yes." Tears escaped her eyes and ran down to wet her shirt. "Yes, and I couldn't do anything. I couldn't move. I gasped and jumped down. My boot hit on the metal of the air-conditioner unit and one of them heard."

"So you got away and came here?"

She bobbed her head. "I had to. And I had to bring Patch with me." Lifting her eyes to Micah, she said, "Patch belonged to Clyde. That's why Patch wanted me to go to the warehouse with him. He knew they had Clyde in there, but I didn't see him the first time. They must have had him hidden."

She put her hand to her mouth and cried. "I could have saved Clyde. I was so shocked and confused, I went back for proof and now I'm an eyewitness to the murder of an innocent man. They know I have Patch, so they know it was me they saw running away that night."

She heaved a sob and shook her head. "I did call the Winter Lake police and I left because Leon controls the police department. He's always hanging out with them. Now I've put your family in danger, so I need you to take me into town tomorrow so I can report these men to the authorities. I won't let them hurt you or your family."

Micah leaned his hands on the table, his knuckles turning white. "We are way beyond that, don't you think?"

Samantha gave up on the tea. "I'm sorry, Micah. I'm sorry my car landed on your property. Rebecca told me what happened to your parents and I'm very sorry about the accident."

"No accident," he said, a bitter edge to his voice. "They were killed by a drunken man in a souped-up car."

She saw the agony in his eyes. "I understand how you feel. It's unimaginable."

He lowered his head. "Everyone tells me it's *Gott*'s will, but sometimes I get so angry. I miss them. And I miss what could have been."

He had to be thinking of the woman who broke his heart.

"You're doing your best," she said softly, hating the etched torment in his expression. Putting away her own woes, she said, "You have to put Emmie and Jed first, as you should. If you can get me to my gramma's house, I can stay there. It's smaller and I can keep watch."

"It's also remote," he retorted. "Isaac and Rebecca live about a half mile away."

"I'll be okay," she said. "Patch will protect me."

"Patch will bark. That doesn't mean he'll be able to stop someone from harming you...or taking you."

Samantha didn't want to think about that. Did he care or was he being kind? "I can handle things now," she insisted even while her pulse jumped with fear. "I'll secure the house and make sure I stay alert."

"You'll need food and sleep and other things you haven't even considered. Not to mention, if any of the community thinks someone has broken into your *grossmammi*'s home, they'll come searching and find you there."

"Don't you want me away from your brother and sister?"

He brushed at his hair and frowned, something she was getting used to. "Look, Samantha, I went back to check your car. Someone has searched it. I mean thoroughly searched in the glove compartment and underneath the seats. They definitely were looking for something. And I want to know what that something might be."

Micah waited for her to continue, hoping she'd be honest with him. Drained and weary, he'd never dealt much with such goings-on. This went bigger and deeper than a few illegal items. Fake luxury items and real guns. A true modern smuggling ring headed up by the man she thought she loved.

He didn't have to live under a rock to know these people would be ruthless in silencing her.

Samantha watched him as if he would shout at her or make more demands. Was she used to that from the man she'd almost married?

When she did speak, her voice was hollow and quiet. "He's sent people after me and they had to have been looking for anything I might have on them. They'd want to destroy my things and leave no trace of evidence or witnesses."

Micah let out a hissing breath. "So you think they want you dead?"

She nodded and got up to go to the sink. "They'll kill me in the same way they killed Clyde, once they've found out who I've told and what I've said. Which is why I can't stay here. These people are dangerous, Micah. I didn't come to you by choice. I have a plan and I need to carry it through."

"If you called the authorities, how are they even still on the loose?"

Fear brightened her eyes. "He's got people everywhere. Somehow, even if he's in jail he'd have them out looking for me. So I can't tell what I saw, so I'll never be able to testify."

"Then you need to keep hiding."

"Not here, not with you and Emmie and Jed. It's too dangerous." She stared at him, her gaze holding him. "You don't want me here. I can tell that."

"I only want to be prepared," he said, feeling contrite about being snappish. "I've been the sole adult figure for Jed and Emmie. Since our parents died, I've always put their needs first."

"I can see that," she replied before washing her teacup and turning back to him. "I certainly understand. My mother was Amish, but she left as soon as she was eighteen and married an English man—my father."

He stood and moved toward her, his hands

at his side. "Is that why you came back here to live with Martha?"

Samantha lowered her head and stared at her sneakers. "I had to come here. I didn't have anywhere else to go. My mother became ill and my father was dead. His parents stopped speaking to him after he married my mother. I never knew that side of my family."

Micah didn't press her for details. "I wish your *grossmammi* was here to help you through this."

Her head came up and she gave him a glimpse of the turmoil she must be going through. "I'm glad she's away from all of this. She suffered enough dealing with my mother."

"Is your *mamm*—?"

"She's well now and remarried. My father died when I was still young and she had a hard time with her grief. Thankfully, she's better now. Much better."

Micah's heart shifted after hearing about Samantha's parents. She'd been through so much. So she must know how he was feeling right about now.

"What can I do, Samantha? You swept in here and changed my day, but it's not in me to send you away when you're in danger."

"I can see that," she said. "You'll do the right thing even when it goes against what you really want to do."

He gave her a weak smile. "Isn't that what we're taught?" He put his hands on his hips, his frown full of confusion. "I saw the truck—the one that tried to run you off the road. From what I could tell, they both got out. I also saw bloody fingerprints inside the truck."

Samantha guessed what that meant. "They're hiding out somewhere until they can sneak away."

"That, or until they can come after you again," he replied.

Her gaze held his, her eyes full of wonder and concern. "Then do what needs to be done. Get me to my gramma's house and I'll take it from there."

They stood there staring each other down

until finally Micah blinked, his whole being suddenly tied and tangled in this woman who'd fallen out of the sky into his yard.

"Let's get some sleep," he said. "We'll decide what to do in the morning. It's too dangerous to leave now anyway."

He went upstairs and left her standing there, but he felt horrible and turned and came back downstairs.

"Is there anything else you need?" he asked, taking time to study her features. She looked as drained as he felt, yet she held her head high.

"No," she said, moving toward the downstairs bedroom, exhaustion cloaking her. Her shoulders slumped, her head down. "I have clothes and toiletries. I'll be fine."

"Finish telling me," he said. "What would these people be looking for?"

"Evidence, as I said earlier," she replied, weariness making the one word harsh. "I have pictures and I have Patch. They know I'm the one who reported them and he'll keep coming after me because I've turned on him and betrayed him."

"I thought he loved you."

"And he thought I loved him. Now that's all over, and trust me, Leon Stanton is the kind of man who doesn't take betrayal very well."

Micah accepted that for now. "Go on to bed. I'll check the doors and windows again. Make sure you lock your bedroom door."

"Thank you," she said, her gaze holding his. "You saved my life."

"Well, I intend to keep doing that," he admitted. "*Gott* had a reason to bring you to us, Samantha. And I have my reasons for wanting to keep you safe."

"Because it's the right thing to do?" she asked as she held the doorknob to her room.

He held off on answering because so many conflicting thoughts moved through his head. "Yes, and because you seem like a *gut* person. Patch likes you, anyway."

"Patch is a little hero. He led me right to the truth that I couldn't see." She smiled at that admission and went in the room and shut the door, the click of the lock echoing throughout the house.

After she'd left the living room, Micah stood in the shadows and listened, wondering if he should take his gun upstairs with him, just in case.

SEVEN

The next morning Samantha dressed in
jeans and a cotton shirt, wishing she had
brought more suitable clothes. She did put
her hair up in a messy bun so she'd look
a little more presentable, as presentable as
she could be after not sleeping at all. Every
creak and pop of this old house had set her
teeth on edge. She heard imagined sounds,
thinking footsteps were pounding toward
her. Why did she feel as if someone was
standing near the bedroom window in the
middle of the night?

Putting that image out of her mind, she
mustered up her courage and went into
the kitchen to see if she could help. Micah
rushed around making toast and eggs, and
Patch followed his every footstep. Micah's

hair was mussed and he looked like he hadn't slept much either.

When she glanced over at the fabric-covered couch and saw a pillow and blanket, she realized Micah had slept down here.

That gesture touched her heart and told her he was a good man who would do what he had to do.

She would follow suit and get to the authorities as soon as possible.

"Good morning," Samantha said. Patch immediately ran to her, yelping and lunging up on his hind legs. "I had food for Patch in the car. Did you find it?"

"Morning." Micah kept right on with scrambling eggs. "In the mudroom with his food bowl and water dish."

The twins came running down the stairs, startling Samantha even though she could hear them thundering.

"Slow down," Micah said, admonishing them with one of his frowns. "Eat, then go and do your chores. I'll be helping you today."

He sent Samantha a glance on that comment. He'd be too concerned to let the children roam freely right now.

"Can Patch come?" Emmie asked, grabbing toast.

"He needs to eat and yes, he'll need an outside break," Samantha explained. She hurried to the mudroom and found Patch's dog food. And she also found something else.

The side window had been pried open.

"Micah?" she called, trying to keep her voice steady.

He came across the house and glanced into the small, square room. "What?"

She motioned toward the tiny window near a storage shelf, showing him the chipped paint and splintered wood. The window had been opened about an inch. She felt the warm wind on her skin, but she also felt the fingers of fear creeping down her spine.

Turning to the twins, he called, "Go ahead and eat while I help Samantha feed Patch."

He went to the mudroom door. "Did you hear anything last night?"

She stared at the damaged window. "I thought I heard things all night. I can't be sure." Ignoring the shiver snaking through her nerves, she said, "I wouldn't be here right now if they'd managed to get in." Giving him an appreciative glance, she asked, "How about you? Did you sleep in the living room last night?"

He looked sheepish, the frown again on his tense face. "I couldn't sleep so I came down here. I must have checked the doors five times and some of the windows, too." Shrugging, he said, "I never figured anyone would try to break in this tiny window."

"I can't see how those men could get in. Maybe they peeked in." Studying the window, she added, "Why would they do that?"

He let out a breath. "I came in here this morning and put on my muck boots to go tend the animals. Never even glanced toward that window."

Samantha could understand that. It would have been near dawn when he came in and he probably didn't even turn on a light. The damaged window glared at them now with a sinister gawk. "They didn't make it inside. It is a small window, thankfully."

"They might have been about to enter when they heard us upstairs earlier. The twins sound like a herd of cattle at times."

"Patch didn't bark."

"He was exhausted and could have snoozed right through it if it didn't wake you being so close. He got busy chasing the *kinder* until he smelled breakfast."

Patch yelped a soft reminder that he needed breakfast, too.

Samantha absently fed the impatient dog, then studied the window. "Something scared them off, that's for sure. I'm glad of that."

Micah's gaze swept the room. "Well, it's *gut* that they didn't get in. Or did they? Have you checked your things?"

Samantha moved across the hall into the bedroom. She pulled open the armoire where she'd stored her purse and tote bag. Everything looked in place, but the thought of someone creeping around while she slept sent her mind reeling with apprehension.

Tugging at her purse, she checked for her phone. Still there, along with her laptop. If they'd come in and found this, she'd be dead by now.

She saw she'd had several messages from Dorothea. Listening, she heard the panic in her assistant's voice.

"A warehouse on Leon's property was raided and some men were arrested. He's wanted for questioning but can't be found. Samantha, what's going on? Call me, please."

Her heart hammered against her rib cage like a bird trying to get free. She'd never get the image of Leon beating up a helpless old man out of her mind. Nor could she forget the hiss of a silenced gun and how Clyde had slipped off the chair and fallen in a heap to the floor. Leon *wasn't* in jail. He'd sent those men and soon, he'd come here, too.

"Everything's okay," she told Micah when he came into the room. "I need to call my assistant." She didn't want to share what Dorothea had told her. Not until she had details.

When Micah heard an argument breaking out between the twins, he pivoted back toward the kitchen.

Samantha hurried to watch over Patch, her mind whirling. If the law had discovered the smuggling ring, the news would be all over Winter Lake. She prayed these evil men hadn't bothered her assistant. When she came back into the empty kitchen area, she walked to the open back door and saw the children doing their daily chores. Their banter and discussions echoed from the goat corral. Micah stood with them, his gaze wandering over the fields and woods. He was worried and he had every right to worry.

Samantha took a deep breath and tried to call Dorothea back, but her phone went to voice mail. She didn't dare leave a message.

For now, she had more to worry about. Sending his men was one thing. Leon would be angry that they hadn't brought her back. He was somewhere planning his next attempt to get to her and evidently end her life once and for all.

She stood, staring at nothing, wondering if she'd ever get away from him now. He'd track her for as long as it took.

Patch nosed her leg, so she put on his leash and tied it loosely to the porch post to let him roam around the yard while she sat on the porch steps and prayed.

She'd have to be careful not to have a meltdown around the children. But Micah seemed to read her thoughts.

She spotted Micah walking back from the barn with a tool kit. Watching him, she had to admire his broad shoulders and muscular build. He worked hard and had the muscles to prove it. He had a kind face even if he did frown a lot. He'd had to take on a hard task, that of raising his younger siblings. Is that why he hadn't married? Did he think no one would want to be with him because of his siblings? Or maybe he didn't trust anyone else to help with his responsibilities. The twins indicated he had run off most of the available women in the community.

Emmie and Jed were not horrible children, but some would want their man all to themselves. She thought of Leon, her eyes casting down in shame. He never talked about having children and he claimed he loved animals. He did have several dogs of his own, big Dobermans and German shepherds. Guard dogs?

He'd been married once and he never talked about that either except to say he'd been horribly betrayed. He'd been so suave, such a gentleman. Everyone in town respected him. Now, she could see it all in a different light. Everyone in town *feared* him. He'd used her, taking her love for animals and her need to have someone in her life and manipulating her so subliminally she never saw it coming. She'd almost married a sociopath.

Lowering her head and closing her eyes, she silently wondered why she'd been so naive and gullible.

She'd reasoned that she'd never met a man like Leon and she'd only dated briefly here and there in school and while interning. What did she know of love, except how she'd seen her mother suffer? Leon had made her feel special and needed.

Why had he picked her? Because she wasn't a local and he could control her by bringing stray animals so she'd fall for him? He'd charmed her, coaxed her and made her believe in him.

Now she'd seen his true colors.

Well, she sure had fallen hard. Seeing the brutality and the dangerous look on his face when he'd ordered his man to kill Clyde had ended any infatuation she'd held for the man.

She wondered if he'd ever really loved her at all.

She'd betrayed him. And she feared him now more than ever, but she'd stand her ground, somehow. She could start by trying to find his ex-wife. What had happened there? If she'd married him—

"Hey, are you all right?"

Samantha looked up to see Micah standing on the bottom step, his eyes on her with an intensity that burned like a torch. "I'm fine. Just…trying to absorb what's happened to me. We should talk about me moving on." She was about to tell him that Leon was on the loose and not in jail.

Micah's gaze fell over her face, studying her in the quiet way he'd done yesterday. "You'll stay here."

That had not been a suggestion.

Her heart bumped and shifted while she wished she *could* stay here. "It's too dangerous. I won't do that to you and the children." Touching a hand to his arm, she said, "Micah, I heard from my assistant. She left me a message on my phone. He's not in jail as I thought. He's out there and he will not stop sending his bodyguards after me. Sooner or later, Leon will come here himself."

"I think you need to stay hidden as much as possible," Micah replied. "We can pass this information to the whole community— that I have a visitor. One thing we do around here—we gather anyone in need close. We have our own kind of bodyguards."

"I can't ask that of you or anyone else, Micah. I had planned to drive in and hide at Gramma's place without anyone knowing I was even here."

When he smiled, she shot him an aggravated glare. "Is that so funny?"

"With that bright red car shouting to the world, you planned to sneak in and hide?"

"She does have a barn, you know. I planned to hide the car there." Although Samantha really hadn't thought beyond getting here. "I'll be okay on my own with Patch."

"*Neh*. I won't let an innocent woman go out there alone and on the run. We will figure out something together, Samantha."

His voice went soft on her name and for some reason that small gesture made her heart hurt with a new kind of pain.

"*Denke*," she said, not even realizing she'd spoken it in the Pennsylvania Dutch he understood best.

He stopped near her as he passed into the house. "Say that again."

Just a moment, and one look that spoke volumes before he kept moving.

Cautious and unsure, she followed him,

willing to help with the window while Patch stayed near the porch. "Why?"

"Why what?" he asked, his expression showing the same caution.

"Why do you want me to say *denke* again?"

His frown softened and his eyes turned dark. "I like the way you say it."

Something akin to a lightning bolt hit Samantha in her stomach. Micah's eyes darkened as if he'd felt the same thing.

"Denke," she said again, low and unsure.

"I'll fix the window," he replied, blinking. "And I'll put protective measures on all the downstairs windows."

"An alarm?" she asked, still a bit spellbound by the way he'd looked at her.

"An Amish alarm," he replied. "Sturdy sticks as crossbars. It will be hard to pry the windows open."

"My gramma used those," she said, her heart aching with longing for her grandmother.

Micah gave her a wry smile. "My *mamm* loved Martha. Your *grossmammi* is a kind, respected member of this community. She'll give me a good dressing-down if I let any harm come to you."

Samantha fought back tears. "You're very kind, too, Micah. I do feel protected here and I can never repay you."

They both became silent. Micah watched her, his gaze moving over her face. He blinked and started clearing away slivers of wood.

"I'll also set traps around the windows. An animal trap will have a grown man squealing like a piglet. Watch Patch and don't let him get into one of them. I'll caution Emmie and Jed, too."

"Good plan," Samantha said, admiring his ingenuity.

But would his plans keep them safe enough to stop Leon and his overpaid security guards? She still had to wonder why anyone would try this window instead of some of the bigger ones around the house. When she remembered how she'd woken up wondering if someone had been standing outside, shivers of fear played down her spine.

She followed Micah into the mudroom, the smells of clean laundry and farm-stained clothes a familiar mixture. Still unsettled, she glanced around, seeing neat shelves lined with towels and blankets, soap and other supplies. A hat rack and hanging jackets and rainwear, a row of muck boots. All normal in an Amish mudroom. This damaged window wasn't normal.

Those thoughts niggled at her while she watched the man who'd suddenly come into her life. He didn't need this or deserve this—having to deal with a woman on the run from horrible, dangerous people. But he was a good person.

Micah chiseled at the splintered window-sill until he had it removed, then stood back to assess the damage. After clearing away debris, he measured the window and tested a piece he'd already cut to size.

Finally, he glanced back at her. "Would you like to tell me more about your life, Samantha Herndon?"

Back to business. Maybe she'd only imagined the way he'd said her name earlier.

Maybe she'd only imagined how he seemed to like the sound of her voice. She did owe him some kind of explanation, even if she barely knew the man. Her nerves were shot and she was on edge. No wonder she'd imagined lightning bolts and an acute awareness. The man had saved her life, after all. But she was no longer Amish—the first no-no. And she could think of lots more reasons why her imagination needed to curb its enthusiasm.

Maybe if she told him the truth about her sordid background, the lightning-bolt feeling would go away.

"My mother became an alcoholic after my father died," she said. "She was Amish and he was *Englisch*. She left because they were in love. My grandfather, who is no longer alive, shunned her. Gramma stayed in touch with her, but she had to be respectful of my grandfather's wishes, too."

She handed Micah the hammer and nails he'd placed on the bench by the window. He eyeballed the new facing he'd whittled into shape and jammed it against the space in the window.

"I'm sure that was difficult."

"Yes, horrible. My mom never got over leaving her way of life here. When my father died, she had a hard time with that, too. The guilt of not being able to speak to my grandfather ate at her and so the love my parents had soon splintered. He died of a heart attack at a young age, maybe a broken heart since, even while she loved him completely, she seemed to resent him taking her away."

"That is sad," Micah said as he sanded wood and hammered nails. His gaze hit her again. "It does happen, someone falling for the wrong person or going out in the *Englisch* world only to find it's not what they really wanted."

Was he referring to her leaving and falling for Leon?

Samantha didn't want to figure that out, so she kept talking. "Anyway, after he died, she started drinking a lot. She loved him and missed him and regretted how she'd treated him."

"So she sent you here to live with Martha?"

"Yes, because she had no choice. I was eight when I came here. It was difficult at first. I missed my mom and our life in New York. Gramma was patient and kind in teaching me the Amish ways."

"And our language," he said with a smile.

"*Ja*, for certain sure," she teased back, glad they were on an even keel again.

He worked on the windowsill a bit longer. "Do you ever miss this—being Amish?"

Samantha hadn't thought about that before. A piercing longing hit her square in the chest. "I miss Gramma and how simple things used to be. She taught me about faith and forgiveness and love. We'd pick and can vegetables and make jellies and jams. She taught me how to make freshly baked bread, which I still do sometimes. We loved planting flowers and tending to them. Gramma feels closer to God in her garden, so I have a small garden of my own. She taught me about real life and how to never judge someone. She represents the unconditional love in my life."

He glanced up at her. "Sometimes, it does seem love comes with conditions."

"Yes, and I've seen that firsthand now, unfortunately. I couldn't see Leon placed conditions on everything we did together or even what I did on my own time. I was jogging on his property because he wanted to keep me safe, or so he said. He really wanted to control me. He did that in subtle ways that seemed like concern and love but were really manipulations. Even me jogging on his property—he wanted me to follow the main trail. I ventured to another trail that day and now here I am."

"You see that did not work out for him. You found out the truth." He studied her, compassion in his eyes. "Maybe your instincts and a nudge from the Lord caused you to take a different path in order to see what was right before your eyes."

Samantha thought about that for a moment. Had she been so intent on her work and on all that Leon seemed to offer, that she'd missed the subtle signs that something was off?

"Yes, I did feel a tug to try something different. Odd, but I'm glad I found out. His illegal operations need to end. I wished I'd seen it all sooner."

Micah brushed away sawdust and wood chips, then turned to her, his expression softening. "I think because you were among the Amish for so long, you did learn to be less judgmental and that is probably why you saw the *gut* in this man Leon rather than the bad."

Surprised, she watched him turn to finish up his work, thinking she hadn't helped with the window very much. Also thinking her imagination was still hard at work on being aware of this man. "What about you? Have you ever been in love?"

Micah put away his tools and turned to stare at her. "My life is not up for discussion."

After that sharp statement, she stared

at him and wondered what he was hiding. "And mine is?"

"I needed to know all about the stranger who is now in my home," he replied, his eyes widening. "I believe you are a good person, Samantha. I have to know everything. I've always been the curious sort."

"Really, or are you curious about me, because you don't believe I'm telling the truth?"

He gave her that solemn, unreadable frown that he wore like an armor plate. "You told me all about yourself, but that doesn't mean I have to do the same. Rebecca told you about my parents. I live here with Emmie and Jed and we have a simple life, a routine life on a small farm that I struggle to keep together. What more is there to tell?"

"I think there's a lot more to tell," she retorted, a touch of anger surging through her. "I know the Amish are not known for opening up. I wasn't trying to pry. I really would like to know more about you, too."

Micah shook his head. "*Neh*, I've got work to do."

"I can help," she offered. "I'll put on the wash and make dinner."

"You don't need to do that. I thought I'd take you into town so you can let the police know what all has happened and that this Leon person could still be out there. That's a sure threat."

"I *do* want to get that done and find a place with Wi-Fi for my laptop," she said. "If I stay here, I want to do my part to repay you. And, Micah, I'm going to find a way to get out of this, so you can get on with your life."

"I told you, you can stay. At least for a few days. I have to start the first cut on the alfalfa—after I get your car out of my field. You can help by keeping an eye on the twins."

He gave her a fortress-like glance that dared her to dispute him, then went out the back door at a fast pace.

Samantha stood there with her hands on her hips, watching him. An interesting, stubborn, determined man who thought he had to protect a woman he didn't even know.

Traits she appreciated. Especially now.

EIGHT

An hour later Micah loaded the twins, Patch and Samantha into the buggy. "Here's the plan," he said to Emmie and Jed. You will stay with Jeremiah and Ava Jane Weaver until we're done with town business, *ja*?"

"Ja," Jed echoed. "I love it at their house. Jeremiah fishes with us and he taught us how to swim. And Ava Jane makes the best pies."

Samantha couldn't help her smile. Even with the dark cloud of Leon's threats hanging over her, she enjoyed being with the twins and Micah. Too much. She needed to get on with the business of getting away from Leon. Now she had to be brave in front of the children. They were already afraid someone would come back onto their property.

Micah had suggested she wear a *kapp* to hide her hair and he'd found an old dress one of his cousins had left long ago when she'd come visiting. Samantha had put it on, memories of pins and ties making the transition easy. The dress was too big but it worked for now. The scent of lavender lifted from the worn skirt.

"You'll take care of Patch?" she asked, her heart rate going up as they got out onto the road. She dreaded going around the curve where she'd almost lost her life.

"We will," they said in unison.

Emmie piped up. "JJ is so cute. He toddles after us. And Sarah Rose is my best friend. Eli is older so he's always following his *daed* around. They will love Patch."

Micah had explained that Jeremiah and Ava Jane lived close and he often relied on them to babysit since they had three children—two from Ava Jane's first marriage and a toddler of their own. Ava Jane, a shy, strong woman from the way he'd described her, had been a big help to him after his parents died. She'd offered an open invitation to watch the twins when he needed her.

"Now is one of those times," he'd told Samantha. He explained how Jeremiah had gone away and joined the Navy then how he'd returned and dedicated himself to God and this community. And to Ava Jane, the woman he'd left behind. "He's tough and he's well-trained, but he has made his peace with that life and he left it behind. That doesn't mean he won't step up to help a neighbor."

Earlier, he'd also told the twins they should run to Jeremiah's house if they needed help any time while Samantha was their guest. "If I'm not around and you see strangers nearby, you run and get help. Jeremiah and Ava Jane will know what to do."

Samantha was learning that Micah had a steady, solid support system. She remembered that from her days with Gramma. Everyone helped each other around here, one of the special things about a tight community. That also meant everyone always knew each others' business, too. She worried about that, but she needed some advice.

"We'll talk to Nathan Craig about this," Micah had also told her. "He is *gut* about tracking people and figuring out how things can go wrong." Then he added, "He also used to be Amish and now he is happily married to Alisha—she's a lawyer and often helps our community."

Now, updated about the people who worked and volunteered at the Campton Center, she felt better. She had people in her corner. Maybe they could help her fight off Leon, after all.

When they came up on the curve, she gasped and glanced over at Micah. "The truck's gone," she said under her breath.

"Maybe our intruders are gone, too," he replied.

Samantha wished that could be true. She gasped. "We can see if a tow truck picked it up. Track it back to that somehow to build our case."

Micah shook his head. "Now you're thinking beyond being afraid," he said. "That is a *gut* idea."

"If it helps end this nightmare, I'm all for it," she replied.

A few days later, Samantha had settled into a routine that seemed easy in some ways, but difficult considering why she was here. After talking to the local authorities and telling them Leon was at large, Samantha didn't hold out much hope. The township police headquarters was mostly a two-person operation with some part-time patrol personnel. Captain Frank Schroder had assured her they would make the rounds along the main road near Micah's house. When she asked if they'd keep her presence here quiet, they'd agreed—unless the New York police called them to verify.

The captain, an older man who seemed suspicious of everything she told him, stared at her and asked, "Are you sure you didn't just have a fight with your boyfriend and now that you're stuck here, you're jumping to conclusions?"

"I'm telling the truth," she said. "Call the authorities in Winter Lake and get a report. It should match everything I've told you. You have the pictures I took, too."

He scratched his head. "If I call, they'll know you're hiding here."

She wasn't sure she could trust the police captain. "Look for the story in the papers. I'm sure it made headlines in New York."

Nathan Craig, a private investigator whose parents lived not far from town, had talked to her at the Campton Center about how he helped Amish in trouble. He planned to go over her statement and do his own investigation. He asked a lot of questions about all of the happenings around Micah's house and about her life with Leon back in Winter Lake.

"Anything you can tell me about his habits, his past, would help."

"He was married before," she'd told Nathan. "I don't know where his ex-wife is or how to locate her. He never talked about her much. Never called her by name." Samantha thought about her time with Leon.

"He knew everyone in town and now that I look back, he seemed well-respected. Now I can see that it wasn't respect. It was fear. He often hiked alone in the woods, too. Probably to check on his illegal operations."

"We'll figure this out and try to keep you safe," Nathan had promised. "I'll get on this and see which tow truck they used to pull the truck out of the ditch. Sometimes it's easier for someone like me to ask questions instead of the officials snooping around."

After Nathan and she had finished their meeting, Jewel, dressed in a floral sheath and dangling red earrings, had introduced her to Bettye Willis and Judy Campton. Jewel worked at the Campton Center, part bouncer and part assistant to Bettye and Judy.

The three women had spoiled her with a tour of the place and cookies to take back to the twins. "Micah is the best," Jewel had told her. "But if you need a bodyguard, you call me."

On the ride home, she'd gone over everything with Micah. "I've caused quite a stir, coming back here."

"Well, you're here now and we're all aware of it," he'd said. "This community takes care of its own."

Now Samantha had grown used to the whole community watching out for her, but she was still on high alert. How could she rest with Leon out there plotting to get even with her?

Staying busy had helped. She watched each day as Micah and some other workers went through the far end of the alfalfa field with a team of sturdy draft horses, tilling the budding green plants. He'd return the help with their farm work when they needed him. Since she loved to bake, she'd made pies and cookies and she'd managed to cook a passable pot roast with potatoes and carrots. She planned to try making bread, too. It had been a while since she'd made bread from scratch.

Appreciating the indoor plumbing, she had learned to take quick baths and get out of the mudroom before the others came storming in to peel away muck boots and dirty clothing. She'd also enjoyed washing the handmade clothes and she'd managed to use the wringer-style washing machine. Hanging them on the clothesline by the back door was easy and the fresh air and sunshine made them smell wonderful. That scent caused her to long for her grandmother.

She kept reminding herself that memories were coloring the longing in her heart. She missed her gramma, not this way of life. Or was it more than that?

Fear and exhaustion had her doubting herself and wondering what life would be like here with Micah and the twins. Being on constant watch only worsened the situation.

Micah's protection measures seemed to be working so far. No one had tried to break in and he hadn't found any footprints around the downstairs windows. The animal traps were still set. She knew Micah watched the barn and woods all day long and that he often went out late at night to check, taking his hunting rifle with him. He let the twins do their chores, with him nearby to keep an eye on things.

They both existed on a heightened degree of tension.

Or maybe that was from being around each other. Since they shared meals, talked more after the twins went to their rooms and often discussed what each day would bring, they'd gotten into a comfortable routine. A routine that couldn't last.

All through the community, people were still cleaning up after the tornado. That had kept Micah coming and going to help as needed. People had been by here to help, too. They'd cleared out trees and mended fences, fixed the roof shingles, and touched up any damage to the house and barn. Some had been curious about the car that still sat embedded in the muddy field.

Everyone wondered about the woman who'd been staying at the King house. So much for hiding out. So far, no one here had bothered Samantha. They had too much to worry about while rebuilding after those fierce winds had damaged so much property.

Right now, Micah was at the kitchen table, going over some paperwork. Farm life demanded a check-and-balance of the constant stream of money in and money out. He didn't look too pleased. Samantha covertly watched as the line between his eyebrows grew deeper.

He'd done so much for her over the last few days. Today, he planned to gather some men to move her car into the back of the barn. While he'd gone about his work, Samantha had managed to go back over the files she'd saved on her laptop. She had enough battery left to do that and some to spare, since she'd only opened it once. She needed to do some searches on Leon Stanton's past, too. Especially his first wife. Even with Nathan looking around, she still wanted to know more. She'd have to go into town again and use the Campton Center's secure Wi-Fi. Her phone needed recharging, too.

So far, she hadn't found very much beyond his family history. Early settlers in upstate New York on the land he now owned.

A distinguished family. No mention of his wife or his past other than he attended Yale University.

Leon had probably wiped some of his personal information away for good. Or it was at least so buried that she'd never find anything.

"I'm going to check on Emmie and Jed," Micah said, giving her that intense stare she'd come to recognize.

"Okay," she said, aware that she'd been watching him and he'd noticed.

He left, probably needing some air and to be away from her.

A few minutes later a knock at the front door caused Patch to race up onto the porch and bark. Samantha had left him near the porch so she could keep an eye on him. She rushed to untie his leash from the porch railing and then lifted him into her arms. As she glanced toward the barn, she saw the children cleaning stalls. Since school was out for the summer, they had extra chores to keep them occupied.

Micah must have heard the knock or seen

someone turning into the drive. He came back inside and stalked to the door while she waited near the back. "It's Rebecca," he called to Samantha.

Seeing the twins frolicking with the goats, Samantha breathed a sigh of relief. "Patch," she said, unleashing him and putting him down, "go to Emmie." She waved to Emmie and pointed to Patch.

Emmie came running to meet the little dog.

Samantha felt better, knowing he'd bark an alert if anyone unusual came toward the twins.

She hurried into the living area to greet her new friend.

Rebecca held a cloth tote bag in her arms. "*Gut* morning, Samantha. I brought some clothes. Since you used to be Amish, I thought maybe you'd feel more comfortable in these." Glancing at the old dress Samantha had washed several times, Rebecca shook her head. "And I can see I got here not a moment too soon."

"Denke," Samantha said, the word coming naturally to her now.

Micah nodded, appreciation in his eyes. "That was kind of you, Rebecca. If she is to hide out here, she will need to look Amish. I'm pretty sure she's tired of wearing my cousin Ruth's old dresses."

"So you're hiding out still?" Rebecca asked. "I figured as much from the *blabbermauls*."

"Yes." Samantha wouldn't lie anymore, so she gave Rebecca the short version of the latest update. "I don't want to stay here, but Micah is concerned about me leaving. I was on my way to my gramma's house the other day when the storm hit. I wanted to hide there, since I knew she might be at her sister's house."

"And you landed here instead," Rebecca surmised, understanding in her eyes now. "If you hadn't crashed into Micah's field, you might not be alive today. Isn't that interesting?"

"More like, it's too exciting for my boring existence," Micah said. "I don't think she needs to be alone. Some unsavory people are after her."

Samantha took the clothes, his words piercing her soul. He was only being kind, keeping her here. She needed to remember that. "I appreciate your help," she told Rebecca, "but I intend to move on soon."

"If you're in danger, we can help you," Rebecca replied. "You can still come and stay with Isaac and me. We have a large house and rarely have visitors."

Samantha eyed Micah, then looked back at Rebecca. "I'll stay here for now. Maybe they won't return because they know we're aware of them. Micah has taken precautions and we've alerted law enforcement. If anything else happens, I'll move to your house. Sooner or later, I have to face the authorities back in New York, too. I was the whistleblower on this operation and I know the authorities raided their storehouse. Other than calling in what I'd seen, I didn't talk to the police there before I left. They'll need to hear my statement."

She didn't add that the FBI would have

been called in on this, too, since as far as she could tell, this was a federal offense. Leon was still out there somewhere, just biding his time.

Micah's frown increased. "We're keeping watch and I've secured the house. If she dresses Amish, that will help her to blend in."

Rebecca's shrewd gaze landed on Micah. "I can tell it's useless to argue with you, but word might get out and the bishop will *kumm* calling."

"I have not done anything wrong," Micah said with a shrug. "I only helped someone in need. And today, I plan to get help moving her car. It's like a beacon out there."

Rebecca didn't push the issue. "I came with Isaac. He's out pondering the best way to move the vehicle."

Micah lifted his chin in a nod. "One more will help when the others arrive. I can't get it to crank so we'll have to hook the draft horses to pry it out of the ground."

When he heard Jed calling his name, Micah rushed out the back door. Isaac was indeed standing with the twins, Patch in his arms. That little dog could sense the goodness in a person. As well as the evil.

Samantha watched Micah go out and made sure the children were okay before she turned back to Rebecca. They showed Micah and Isaac some fresh tomatoes from the garden.

"What's his story?" she asked, wishing she didn't need to know so much. "He seems to want to protect me, yet he also seems to resent me being here and bringing danger on his family."

"That one—he was engaged to a pretty girl. When his parents were killed and buried, that pretty girl suddenly didn't want to be his wife anymore."

"Why not?" Samantha asked, her mind forming a scenario since Emmie had mentioned his girlfriend had run off with another man.

"He told her the *kinder* would be part of the package, that he could not abandon them," Rebecca said. "And she did not like that idea."

"So she broke things off?"

"She did and a few months later, she found a new man from another community and left Campton Creek. I'm afraid her standards were outside the realm of being Plain."

"She jumped the fence?"

"Over it and gone. She lives in the *Englisch* world now."

Samantha turned to watch Micah with his siblings. Things made more sense now. She'd left and joined the English world, like the girl he wanted to marry. No wonder he wasn't so sure about having her around.

Right now, he looked almost relaxed as he talked to Isaac and watched the twins. They were laughing and chasing the baby goats, Patch falling right in step. It was such a sweet, peaceful, normal scene, her heart leaped toward them with a deep longing.

"I can't imagine any woman telling her fiancé that, so it sounds as if this one already had one foot out the door. Now I understand what he's really been going through.

He loves his family and he'll always put them first."

"He does, for certain sure," Rebecca said. "He blames himself for his parents' deaths, so I'm guessing he is trying to make up for that with saving you. A good heart, but a confused head. I don't normally gossip. I thought you'd need to know who you're dealing with."

Samantha took that as a gentle warning.

"Thank you for telling me, Rebecca. It only reinforces what I've said all along. I can't stay here."

Rebecca put her hands on her hips. "What if Micah seems to like having you here? He's tenacious when it comes to protecting others. He feels responsible, but this is different."

Samantha couldn't hide her blush. "He's trying to help—that's all."

"*Ja*, and he's got you to help with the cooking and cleaning and taking care of Emmie and Jed. I'm thinking this is about more than protecting you. Best be aware of everything that's going on here, ain't so?"

Samantha couldn't answer her friend. She knew there could never be anything more between Micah and her.

NINE

After Isaac went to his buggy to get some tools, Micah watched the twins playing with the baby goats. Patch yelped and tried to keep up, causing them to giggle even more. Their laughter always brought music to his ears and these days he had to stay close to them. The extra stress of that and having Samantha here, added to keeping up with the growing crops, gave him a daily headache.

Samantha and Rebecca came outside and headed to the small corn patch. "We'll have creamed corn for supper," she called in passing. She glanced at the twins, worry in her eyes, too.

Micah watched as she and Rebecca went to the edge of the cornfield to pull a few ears of corn from the silky green stalks.

Gathering the corn and shredding the stalks would come later in the year, at least.

He should send her away with Rebecca and get back to normal, but for some strange reason he wasn't ready to let her go. The twins liked her well enough and they obviously loved little Patch. While it was strange, having a female in the house made his life seem more settled and normal. Maybe he should consider meeting up with one of the casserole ladies.

No. He wasn't ready and right now, he was dealing with one lady who both puzzled and intrigued him. More pressure would only make him more anxious. He also felt obligated to protect her since she'd crashed on his property.

The danger was real. He didn't want Samantha or his brother and sister to get hurt or worse. Glancing out to where her car sat hunched against the green field, he saw images he couldn't get out of his mind. He'd rounded up some neighbors to help move it. They'd be here soon. Micah was glad for that, since the car reminded him of how his heart had dropped the day the tornado had hit and he'd seen Samantha's deathly pale face covered with blood.

It was only natural he'd want to protect her.

You can't protect everyone.

He'd tried so hard to be a good son and he'd failed so miserably. He'd been arguing with his *daed* and *mamm* the night they died. He'd refused to get in the buggy with them to go pick up the twins from a neighbor's house.

Instead, he'd gone on foot to another house to visit with the girl he'd been walking out with—the girl he'd hoped to make his wife.

In a matter of days, he'd lost his parents and the girl.

He wouldn't go down that road again. Chastising himself for even thinking along those lines about a woman he'd been forced to take into his home, he knew it was wrong, plain and simple.

The Amish usually kept such things to themselves when it involved one of their own, but now outsiders had brought danger to his home. He had to let the authorities do their work.

Lost in his thoughts, Micah heard a distant roar, a buzzing like a motor running or a plane flying low in the sky.

Emmie stopped running.

Jed pointed to the clouds.

Isaac came around the corner and stopped to stare.

Samantha looked up, one hand over her eyes as she stared into the bright sun.

Then she dropped the bundle of corn and screamed, "Run! Emmie, Jed, run!"

The children started shouting and took off toward the house. Patch barked and followed. Isaac made it to the porch and shouted for Rebecca.

Rebecca hurried away, calling to Samantha. *"Kumm!"*

Micah ran to meet the twins, then he saw it.

A drone—something the *Englisch* used now as toys and to spy on others. They sometimes flew over Campton Creek, then posted things on social media, or so he'd heard. This one hovered toward the field and outbuildings. It turned, now heading straight toward where Samantha stood frozen.

The drone approached and went low. Emmie looked back, tripped and fell. She screamed and clawed at the dirt to get up again. Samantha came alive and rushed out to grab Emmie, half dragging her toward the house, Jed sprinting behind them.

Samantha pushed Emmie. "Go, run." She turned, the drone hovering over her head.

Emmie screamed for Jed. "Hurry, *bruder*!"

Micah went into action and raced toward the twins, shouting at them. Samantha turned toward Jed, but Micah reached her and shoved her to the ground, trying to cover her while he shouted for Jed to hurry.

The buzzing spiderlike gadget hovered over them. Micah braced himself, not knowing what would happen. Samantha held tightly to him, her eyes a misty fog of fear and regret.

The drone abruptly whirled and dived toward Samantha's embedded car. A flash of fire hit the car and a roaring boom rattled the earth. Fire and shrapnel sailed up into the air, fragments coming close to where Micah and Samantha lay on the ground.

Micah looked back to make sure the children were safe. Rebecca and Isaac huddled with them on the porch. Micah looked down at the woman in his arms.

Samantha stared up at him, her eyes dull with shock now, and her heart pumping. "Is everyone all right?" she asked on a shaky breath.

He turned, sat up and then nodded, his chest heaving as he scanned the yard and house. "The twins and Patch are on the porch with Rebecca and Isaac." Then he pointed. "Your car is badly damaged."

Samantha struggled to stand, so he took her hand and helped her up. She pivoted and gasped, her palm going to her forehead. "They blew up my car."

"With a drone," he added as he stomped to the pump and grabbed a water bucket.

"Samantha, they were coming for you. These people are serious."

"I told you." She pushed at her tumbled hair, running to catch up, Isaac hurrying behind her. "I told you. Leon owns tech stock and he knows all about the latest technology. He uses drones on his property for security. I've watched him test this kind—a laser drone. Now he's brought them to spy on me."

"Not just to spy," Micah shouted. "To do harm to you."

The rage in her eyes radiated a swift heat that matched the fire about to spread over the field. "They could have killed Emmie and Jed."

"I am well aware of that," he said as they watched her car going up in flames while he pumped water. The field had dried out since the storm and the grass, leftover twigs and small limbs could easily burn. "I have to put that fire out before it spreads."

"I'll help." She grabbed another bucket and filled it. The bucket of water was heavy, but she practically ran to the vehicle, huffing as she moved.

Isaac did the same. "Are you all right?" he asked Micah in passing. Micah nodded and rushed with his own bucket to the fire.

"Samantha, be careful," he shouted. "If the gas tank is damaged it could get worse."

Ignoring him, she heaved the bucket and threw water over the hissing flames. Micah did the same, frantically stomping against the ground around the car so the green grasses wouldn't burn even more. The flames grew because of the leaking gasoline.

Isaac moved back to the well, then turned. "Micah, get away!"

They were heading back with more water when the fire hissed and spewed. Micah could hear the roar.

Taking Samantha's water bucket, he tossed it toward the explosion before grabbing her hand and running with her.

Another boom echoed over the countryside and caused them both to hit the ground. Micah cringed, but still held her hand, his ears ringing with a roaring buzz after the boom had died down.

Samantha turned and scooted back from the intense heat. "It's spreading," she said, pulling her cell phone out of her pocket. "I'm calling for help."

Micah didn't stop her. He managed to stand, then went running to get more water. The twins and Isaac rushed out.

"Can we help?" Rebecca shouted from behind them.

Micah threw water into the raging heat, but it was hopeless. "*Neh*, get them back, Isaac. Stay back."

When they heard sirens, his relief was short-lived. This would be all over the community. Now Samantha would be completely exposed. The pump truck might be able to save his hay crop. He knew, by law, they'd have to report this. Samantha would be in even more danger. And so would his family.

If Micah had ever doubted it, he now realized that having Samantha here might cause problems worse than this one. How could he protect her against this kind of evil force?

"Denke," Micah told Jeremiah and the other men who'd come to put out the fire. "I need to go and talk to Captain Schroder again."

"You know we had to report the drone strike," Jeremiah said, his deep blue eyes full of questions. "A drone is a rare thing around here, especially one that uses a laser to destroy a vehicle, so this might go above our understaffed police department." Glancing over at the burned mass, he added, "And one that has the force of a mini rocket takes it to another level."

"Having a woman's car land in your field is a rare thing, too," Micah replied, soot and dirt all over his clothes. "They were aiming for her, but went for the car. I guess if they couldn't kill her, they want to trap her here, and also expose her to the community. They have succeeded at both."

"Or make a statement that they'll keep

coming," Jeremiah said. "What's going on, Micah?"

Micah gave him a brief update on how Samantha wound up here. "I was afraid to let her leave."

Jeremiah listened with the intensity that Micah had come to know over the years, then nodded. "The firemen know the drone was the source of the blast. The explosion probably knocked down the drone so that can hold some answers if they find it. I can tell you such an attack has to be well planned and calculated. Whoever did this knows what he's doing."

"A laser. What next?" Micah asked. Jeremiah had gone off for twelve years and had served the country in the military. He didn't mess around.

Jeremiah gently slapped him on the back. "Be completely truthful with the police, Micah. They need to know every detail. This is dangerous stuff."

"I'll tell them what I know," Micah said. "And I hope Samantha will do the same."

He left Jeremiah to the task of sorting

things out and walked toward where Samantha sat on the back of an open ambulance, Rebecca by her side.

"Are you all right?" he asked when the two women looked up.

Samantha pushed away the light blanket the paramedics had given her. "Other than a few surface burns on my arm and a dull ringing in my ears, I'm fine. The twins have been checked over and are inside with Isaac and Patch."

She studied his face, her gaze moving to his burning cheek. "You have another cut."

"I'd gotten over the one from...the tornado," he said, his heart bursting with some unknown emotion. "I'll have scars."

Samantha didn't say anything. They both knew some scars went deep.

"Isaac is okay, thankfully," Rebecca said. "I'm grateful he got out of the way in time. First the storm and now this. You'll have more people snooping around to see what's up." Eying both of them, she got up. "I'll go check on him and the *kinder*, then make some lemonade for the fire people."

After Rebecca left, Samantha sat with her hands against her stomach. "I'm sorry, Micah. I've told the captain and the patrol officer everything about what happened today. They have Leon's name and his address already and they've verified that I'm from Winter Lake. I told them about the intruders who've been on the property and now this, of course. I also told them Leon is an expert on the latest technology. This drone had to have come straight from him. He's fascinated by those things and I'm thinking he probably had a storehouse of this type of weapon, possibly selling them on the black market."

"Did you share that with the police?"

She nodded. "They'll check into everything I'd told them, but they have limited resources. Even if they find the drone, they'd have to send it to a state lab for testing."

She stopped and lowered her voice. "I've given them the photos I took and the notes I jotted down. Nathan has that information, too, because I feel I can trust him. Surely the police can use what I heard and saw to prove what the authorities in New York have found."

"If they raided the warehouse, they have proof," Micah replied. "If they can't find the ringleader, that's another matter. He's threatening you, but he's also hiding."

"He has people who'd do his bidding." She shrugged. "I'm afraid to trust law enforcement. Leon ruled over the police in our town. What if he's reached out to someone here?"

"What if you gave up all that information and he has paid someone off? The local police can only do so much to help protect you. They're not used to this kind of crime, Samantha. How can I be sure those people won't return?" he asked, wishing he didn't feel so torn. Wishing he had better ways to protect her.

"Because I'm leaving," she said, pushing to stand. "I should have kept going once I landed here. I felt safe here, but that was an illusion. Or more like a delusion. Leon will keep coming until he kills me. He's got something to prove and if that means eliminating me, so be it."

"Where will you go?"

She gave him a soul-crushing stare. "Rebecca insists I go to their house, and she'll get the word out that I'm no longer staying at your home. I told the police I'd be leaving your place. They didn't seem to believe anything I told them. Maybe that will get back to Leon and he'll leave you alone, at least."

"Do you think they'll even investigate this further?"

"They have to—only to see if I'm imagining things."

"What did they say about connecting with New York?"

"That they've spoken to the police in Winter Lake and they can substantiate what I've told them. The authorities in Winter Lake want me to come back since the captain felt obligated to tell them I'm here. They said they'd protect me. The police here seem to agree that I should go back."

"I don't believe that," he replied with too much force. "I had to deal with our police when my parents died. Captain Schroder wanted to blame my folks for being on the road after dark. That's how things are sometimes. If you go back there, who's to say this man Leon doesn't run their payroll."

"I'm sorry for what you had to go through, Micah," she replied, understanding in her eyes. "I might not have any choice. They'll want me as a witness if they can pin anything on Leon. I can only tell them the facts."

"He might be behind their suggestion that you return there. I don't think you should do that."

"I don't plan on going back unless I have an official escort and protection."

Micah looked down at her and saw the apprehension mixed with regret in her eyes. "I wish we could have met under different circumstances," he said. "If you were still Amish—"

"I'm not," she replied, her eyes widening with the realization that he'd already felt in his heart. "I'm not that girl anymore."

He nodded. "Let's get you inside. I'll help Jeremiah and the others where they need me."

Samantha took one last look at what used to be her vehicle. "I had such dreams," she said on a raw whisper. "I thought I'd met the man God wanted me to be with. Leon sure presented himself in the best light—deacon at the church, animal lover, good man who helped others, a pillar of the community. All the right facades, while his soul is as rotten as dead leaves. He's a sociopath of the worst sort and he's an evil man. How can I ever get past that to trust again?"

Micah walked with her toward the house, keeping a respectable distance when he wanted to hold her and comfort her.

"You can trust me, Samantha. No matter what, remember that."

She gave him an appreciative smile. "I'll remember, Micah."

Then she walked into the house, her shoulders hunched and her head down.

Micah had been sincere in what he'd said, but could he ever trust another woman to be a part of his life? What could he do about Samantha? Not that it mattered.

She'd go back to her life when this was over and he'd be here, trying to live the life *Gott* had given him.

It was well and good that she'd be leaving his home.

"We'll leave at dark," Rebecca told Samantha later that day.

Isaac left to go check on things at their place. He'd be back to pick them up. Emmie and Jed were finishing chores before nighttime, Micah with them. "We'll keep you hidden. We'd do anything for Micah." Giving Samantha a thorough once-over, she smiled. "You look so natural in your Amish clothes it might be easier than I realized to keep you hidden. You'll blend right in."

Samantha thought her friend could be right. She'd gone back to the old ways without too much effort, but did she want to truly return? Her life was in shambles right now. Once she knew Leon and his minions were behind bars, she'd have to make some hard decisions. It would be easy to stay in the shelter of this quiet community, only she couldn't hide out the rest of her life.

"I don't want to trouble you and Isaac," Samantha said after they'd made sandwiches for the firemen and others who'd worked to remove the blackened remains of her car from the field once they'd established the explosion's source and verified the cause of the fire. "I'm pretty sure the bishop won't like any of this."

"Isaac has already explained to Bishop King. He's a very understanding man and he wants no harm on any of us. You were once Amish and he respects that you find comfort in coming home. Martha carries a lot of respect with all of us." She stopped and looked directly at Samantha. "This latest attempt might change his mind on that, however. Do you think we should let your *grossmammi* know you're here?"

Samantha didn't want her gramma involved. "I'm afraid to bring her back. But I sure do need her."

"I can write to her," Rebecca offered. "Or have someone call her."

Samantha didn't say no. "Let's hope the police will be able to coordinate things with the New York authorities, and probably the FBI, too, at that, and bring these people to justice. If that happens, I'll be free from harm and then I can see Gramma again."

Rebecca didn't argue with her. Samantha helped her clean the kitchen, then went to her room to freshen up and pack her clothes. She was almost finished when Emmie came running in.

"We need help, Samantha," the little girl said, tears in her eyes.

Samantha's heart skipped ahead. "What's wrong?"

"One of the kid goats must have gotten scared when your car exploded. He's hung up in the fence and he's crying."

Samantha automatically started to grab her doctor bag, but remembered she'd left it at home. "Let's go," she said. She'd have to do this without modern equipment. "Show me."

"Can you save him?" Emmie asked, her innocence and hope piercing Samantha's soul.

"I'll do my best," she said. Right now, she couldn't make any promises other than that one.

TEN

Micah searched the yard for Samantha and
Emmie. "Jed, where did they go?"

"Maybe in the barn," Jed called from
where he stood feeding the chickens. "Emmie's worried about one of the kids."

He'd warned them to stay close to the
house. Emmie always had to make sure
the baby goats were secure for the day. She
loved playing with them and nurtured them
with motherly concern.

Both of his siblings had been shaken
today. They'd never seen anything like a
drone before and neither had he. Not up
close like that. Watching the contraption
heading toward them had aged him ten
years and made the twins too aware of all
the happenings around here.

Fatigue fell like a heavy coat over Micah.

The firemen were gone for now. Between their efforts and the help of some of the neighboring men, his hay field was still intact. Intact, but with a big black, charred hole right in the middle. The fire department would study the remains of Samantha's vehicle and send reports to the proper authorities. He trusted Jeremiah to be truthful with him.

Now the whole community would be buzzing with the news that a drone had destroyed the *Englischer*'s car. As if he didn't have enough to cause him to worry.

He rushed through the open barn doors and heard Samantha and Emmie laughing in a corner past the livestock stalls. He stopped to watch them and listened in over the neighs and snorts of the big horses and the shuffles of the few cows he kept.

"See, he's okay," Samantha said on a low voice, her silhouette so natural-looking, it was as if she belonged here. "Just a little scratch on his left leg. I've cleaned it with the soap we found by the water pump and he doesn't need stitches. We'll bandage him up with that gauze your brother keeps in the tack room."

"And we can check on him every hour, right?" Emmie said, her sweet voice full of concern.

"Of course," Samantha agreed. "Would you feel better if we bring him onto the back porch? We don't have a kennel and he'd probably run away."

"I don't want that," Emmie said. "I'll check on him until dark and maybe Micah can fix him up a little cage closer to the house." She went quiet then asked, "Will he be safe? I don't want him to be scared again."

Another silent moment. "We will do our best to keep him and all your animals safe," Samantha said, her serene expression belying what she must be feeling inside. "I hope you and Jed and Micah will be okay now, too."

Micah came around the corner, appreciating that Samantha had been so kind to his siblings. Her being here and giving them attention only showed how he sometimes took them for granted and neglected them. He'd have to do better at that. It seemed he never had any spare moments.

"What's this I hear about a sick kid?" he asked, pretending he hadn't heard a word, pretending he hadn't heard the fear and doubt in both their voices. "We do not allow baby goats to get sick around here."

"Micah!" Emmie jumped up and tugged him to the corner where they'd placed the tiny goat in a hurriedly-put-together corral of old wood and a couple old chairs. Lifting the kid out, she said, "He got scared and tried to get through the fence. You need to fix that gap in the left corner."

"What gap?" Micah asked. "That fence is solid. I check it enough to know that."

Samantha sat with her legs tucked under her skirt. "Emmie's right. There is a gap in the fence. As if someone—" she stopped, her gaze shifting up to Micah's "—as if someone didn't notice it needed repairing."

Micah sent her a slight nod of acknowledgment for what she'd almost let slip. Someone had tampered with the fence. "Let me go and check it. You two should stay close to the house. Take the kid with you."

"Are we still in danger?" Emmie asked as she stroked the silky white hair of the squirming kid. "Those bad people are gone now. The police scared them away, didn't they?" Her inquisitive gaze moved from Micah to Samantha. "They won't come back anymore, will they?"

Samantha shot him a beseeching stare. "We are going to make sure that you and Jed are safe. Sometimes bad things happen and we can't make promises that they won't. God is watching over us. We pray that man who tried to break in won't return and no more drones pass by."

"Let's hope not," Micah said, grabbing his pliers and bolt cutters. When he rounded the barn and saw the damage to the wire fence, he knew this wasn't something he'd overlooked and there was no way the storm could have done this damage. Someone had tried to cut through the wiring of the goat corral that extended out beyond their shelter shed.

But why?

Studying the enclosure, he could only guess they hoped to gain access to the barn from the back, maybe to lie in wait for someone to enter? He'd taken this barn for granted, thinking of it as a haven, a place for work and to protect his animals. Now it took on sinister shadows and mysterious creaking noises.

He checked the goat shed and found it clear. No footprints there or anywhere else for that matter. He studied the grass and dirt near where the wire fence met the big barn. Fresh footprints near the cut place in the fence.

Someone had intruded on his property yet again.

Something must have scared them off. Maybe Patch had barked, unknowingly. Or the overprotective does or one of the wethers he kept around had chased the intruder away.

When had this happened? Before or after the drone strike? Had someone hoped to use the explosion as a cover while they entered the barn and hid until nightfall?

Micah did a hasty bandaging of the wires until he could redo the whole section. Goats were notorious about chewing their way through anything, but not this strong wire and these solid, crisscrossed boards.

A human had made these cuts.

Just one more reason to get Samantha to a safer place.

How would he know she was truly safe?

Not your problem, he reminded himself as he headed back to the barn. Taking a glance around, he figured he'd have to check every corner over and over to be sure.

"Let's take your baby up to the house," he suggested to Emmie, his gaze on Samantha. "I have a shipping crate we can use."

After locating the crate and using the search to make sure no one was lurking in the barn, he brought it back to Emmie.

"Get this to the porch. We'll find some blankets to put in there and feed him some hay and a bit of grain. Not too much. He's only been weaned a couple weeks ago. We don't want to upset his stomach."

"Can he hop out?" Emmie asked, oblivious to the tension between Samantha and Micah. "I don't want him to get away."

"It's tall and sturdy enough that he should be okay for a while."

Jed ran up and Emmie told him about the little goat. "We have to take care of him, Jed."

"I'll help," her brother offered. He patted the frightened animal's head.

Micah shooed them along, concern making him gruff. "Go ahead and take him up. Samantha and I will be there shortly."

Micah watched Emmie carry the little goat to the house, his mind seeing grim scenarios while he heard her cooing to the little fellow. Turning to face Samantha, he said, "Someone's been prowling around this barn."

She nodded, distress coloring her eyes. "So all those times the animals were restless means they sensed someone near."

"*Ja*, they always got away before we could discover them."

"This is why I'm leaving, Micah," she said, pushing at her falling-down hair. "Once they finish getting this crate up to the house and get Emmie and her baby goat settled, I'll go. Rebecca is waiting and Isaac should be back by now. I'm sure they're ready to go home."

Micah should be thankful she was going. Instead he worried these people would follow her. Grabbing her hand, he said, "Don't do anything noble or stupid, Samantha. Stay with Isaac and Rebecca. You'll be safe as long as you don't try anything on your own or try to go to your grandmother's place."

"I can't be safe until Leon is behind bars," she said. "I won't continue to put you and Emmie and Jed in the line of fire. And I certainly won't do that to Rebecca and Isaac either."

She took off ahead of him, looking regal in spite of her plain clothes. She also looked natural and at home in those clothes.

Micah shook off the disturbing feelings

that kept nudging at his soul. He had no interest in this woman who'd moved from this world to the *Englisch* world. He needed to remember that.

He had to take care of this land and his siblings. That was more than enough for him. As the sun settled over the distant hills and the shadows of day became hulking and shrouded in darkness, Micah felt a chill passing in the midsummer heat.

Who was in those woods?

Were they watching him even now?

And what if they kept coming long after Samantha had left?

Samantha reached the house in record time and helped Emmie find what she needed for the baby goat. When Rebecca heard her knocking around in the mudroom, the other woman came to stand at the door.

"Is something wrong, Samantha?"

Samantha whirled and nodded. "You mean besides the fact that a madman is trying to kill me?"

"Yes, besides that," Rebecca replied in her serene way.

"I'm sorry," Samantha said after she'd located some old towels and blankets. "That drone strike was terrifying and could have turned out badly. Micah is so angry and I don't blame him. It was unreasonable of me to stay here with strangers when I have a place to hide."

"You can't do this alone," Rebecca said. "You have to see that now."

"The local police already know about me being here and now the whole community will soon know. I'm not safe anywhere, especially not here."

"If you're worried about Isaac and me, don't be," Rebecca replied. "We are watchful and we are careful. There isn't much crime around here. Every now and then some *Englisch* teens decide it might be fun to paint nasty words on our barn. Isaac has ways of finding out about people and he has ways to stop any trespassers."

"Not violent, I hope," Samantha said. "I don't want to bring that down on you."

"No, no violence," Rebecca said. "Just one mean bull and a couple of dangerous male goats."

Samantha actually laughed. It felt so foreign, she stopped short. Taking Rebecca's hand, she said, "You remind me of my grandmother."

"She and I are friends," Rebecca said. "She'd want me to take care of you." Holding tight to Samantha's hand, Rebecca gave her an understanding stare. "I think it's best you come with us, not only because someone is trying to harm you."

Samantha saw the compassion in her friend's eyes. "I agree. It's for the best all the way around."

Because if she stayed here much longer, she'd have to admit her growing feelings for Micah and his brother and sister, feelings that could never develop into anything more than friendship and gratefulness.

They heard a rustling outside. "That would be Isaac," Rebecca said, pivoting toward the front of the house.

Isaac entered and patted his wife's arm.

"Sorry I'm late getting back. I saw two black trucks riding the roads, so I waited as long as I could."

"They're still out there," Samantha said from where she stood near the hallway. "They'll keep coming."

"I'm afraid so," Isaac replied. "We'll need to smuggle you out at dark, to be safe."

Micah came up the hall. "What's going on?"

Isaac filled him in. "We wait here for a while." He scratched his beard. "I went to the phone shanty and called the town police."

Micah got his shotgun and headed for the front door. "I'll be right back."

"Micah, don't go out there," Samantha said. "You don't want to shoot at them."

"My property, my decision," he said as he hurried out the door.

Samantha and Isaac went to the window to watch as Micah approached where the trucks were sitting, his gun lowered. Samantha heard him shout, "Leave now, before the police show up."

The trucks didn't move. Micah walked closer.

A patrol car came around the bend and slowed. Both trucks cranked up and roared away. The officer followed.

Micah came back in and put away the shotgun. His gaze flashed from Isaac back to Samantha. "You're right to leave. Keep moving around and we can throw them off, I hope. I'd go with you tonight."

"You have to stay here," she finished. "Emmie and Jed need you."

He could only nod. It seemed they'd both come to the same conclusion. She was leaving for more reasons than one.

"I'll get her safely to our place," Isaac said. "We'll pretend you are one of our own, Samantha."

The man had no idea how sweet and enticing that sounded to her right now. To be free and clear with no worries of being killed and…to be able to let her feelings for Micah be real.

Were they real? She'd been through so much these past few days, the kind of life-changing trauma that could make a person's perspective shift and become disoriented and distorted. She wasn't prepared for these strong emotions he brought out in her. Way too soon after Leon to feel so impulsive. Maybe like the animals she loved, she'd attached herself to the human who had saved her and was now protecting her. Micah stirred long-held emotions and so did Campton Creek.

She did feel at peace, being back here. As much at peace as she could be with Leon sending people to kill her.

When had this happened? This longing inside her soul.

Probably a natural reaction to Leon's evil ways and how he'd used her and lied to her.

Here, she felt safe and welcome. Here, people looked out for each other and didn't keep dangerous secrets as she'd had to do.

Soon, she'd have to leave this cocoon and go back out into the real world.

She was moving on for the sake of the

man studying her so intently right now. She had a feeling her leaving couldn't be soon enough for him.

ELEVEN

Since the two pickup trucks had left once they saw a patrol car cruising by, Isaac and Rebecca got Samantha into the buggy by bringing it close to the house. Rebecca and Samantha left together, keeping their heads down as they rushed to the buggy. They couldn't be sure if the pickups had been construction workers parked out beyond the farmhouses or Leon's men watching Micah's house.

Either way, Samantha only knew she had to leave, and she hoped that by doing so, Micah and the twins could get back to a normal routine. She and Patch would miss them so much.

Rebecca settled on the buggy seat and turned to give Samantha a reassuring smile. "We'll be there soon."

Samantha sat in the back, out of sight, her mind swirling with an ebb and flow of so many rising emotions. She'd hugged Emmie and Jed and pushed back tears when Patch whined to stay with the twins.

"We'll visit him," Micah had told her once she'd decided to take the dog. Leaving him here would indicate she was still here.

"Patch would like that," she said. "And so would I." She turned to Emmie and Jed. "I'll let you visit with him, either here or wherever I am. Soon."

It was the only thing she could promise and even that might not happen.

The twins accepted her promise, their eyes full of trust.

Emmie hugged her and said, "You'll come back to visit, won't you?"

Samantha had glimpsed at Micah. "I for sure will visit. You are all so special to me."

Micah had followed them to the door. "Stay safe. I'll drop by and check on you when I can."

Samantha could only nod. She'd thanked him over and over.

As the buggy pulled away, she closed her eyes and said a prayer for Micah and his family. She'd miss them, no doubt about that. Danger and a storm had brought them together.

Or maybe God had done that. She wasn't sure.

"You know we live close to your *grossmammi*, Samantha," Isaac said now. The big horse tugged the buggy toward home.

"Good to know," she replied, wondering how she'd ever find her way home. Winter Lake didn't seem so bucolic and peaceful now. "I need to get in touch with my assistant," she blurted. "I left her in charge of my practice and I'm concerned about her."

Rebecca nodded and looked around at Samantha. "We can take you into town in the morning. We usually go in for supplies at the Hartford General Store. Mr. Hartford has a little office in the back and he lets us use his phone as needed. I'm sure you can charge your fancy laptop while we shop."

"I'll appreciate that," Samantha said, glad she'd be able to take some action. That would keep her mind off worrying and feeling helpless, at least. "I need to be my own advocate on this situation."

"Don't advocate yourself into a corner," Rebecca replied. "These people coming after you seem to be very determined."

Samantha could only nod. Exhaustion dragged at her like a chain. Her life had been turned upside down and she wasn't sure how to get it back on track. She'd had the perfect job, the perfect man—or so she thought—and a content life. But had she really been content with Leon and his demands? Or had she settled because she was afraid to be cast aside again in the way her mother had cast her aside?

They were clopping along when headlights shined brightly behind them. Samantha came back to the present and turned and looked through the tiny back opening of the buggy, the lights of the big vehicle blinding her. Sliding down, she said, "I think one of the trucks is back."

"I believe you are correct," Isaac said. "Let's stay calm and hope they pass."

Samantha took another peek, her heart racing, her temples throbbing with fear and adrenaline. "They're getting closer."

"Hold on," Isaac said as the engine of the big truck roared to life. He moved off the road a bit, giving the truck an opportunity to pass.

The truck held back, staying behind.

"Let me out," Samantha said, breathless. "I'll run through the woods so you two can get away."

"We will do no such thing," Rebecca said. "We won't leave you to the mercy of these evil people."

Isaac eased back onto the road and picked up the pace, the reins popping right along with the click of his tongue to his teeth.

Once more, the truck eased up close to the buggy's back side. Samantha took a breath and prayed with all of her heart. Isaac and Rebecca shouldn't be a part of her drama, and yet they were willing to help her.

Please, dear Lord, don't let this happen. Not to them.

She thought of Micah and the twins and

how they'd lost their parents. She couldn't allow them to lose Isaac and Rebecca, too.

"My phone," she said, urgency in the words. "I can call for help." She quickly dialed 911 and told the dispatcher someone was tailgating their buggy.

The truck stayed on them, pulling up close then backing away. Samantha silently screamed for the police to hurry, hurry.

"We'll be home soon," Isaac said. "They might follow us in."

Samantha would hop out of the buggy and surrender before she'd let that happen. She was about to do that when she looked back and saw flashing lights.

"The police are here," she said, her breath rushing out.

The truck took off around the buggy, peeling rubber.

Isaac again pulled over to let the patrol car by. It went after the truck, lights still flashing.

After it was over, Isaac stopped inside their driveway. "You ladies all right?"

"We are *gut*," Rebecca said, reaching

back for Samantha's hand. "I'm thankful you had that phone and thought to use it."

"So am I," Samantha replied, squeezing Rebecca's hand.

Soon they were pulling into the short lane that led up to a neat, trim white house with a big front porch and a small barn behind it. She couldn't tell much in the dark, but part of a wooden fence had been mended. Probably damaged from the storm. The whole place was small and more enclosed, not like Micah's huge sloping yard and wide fields beyond.

Isaac turned to her. "I'll pull the buggy up to the back porch and drop you two off."

"Be careful," Rebecca cautioned her husband. "Someone could be hiding in the barn."

Isaac nodded. "I'm aware, wife. I'm aware."

Rebecca guided Samantha up the two steps to the small porch. "I think we're safe. It's dark and we covered you as much as possible and hid you in the back of the buggy. Who knows if that truck dropped someone off here. We'll check the downstairs and I'll show you the upstairs bed-room where you'll be staying." Patting Patch, she added, "Because you are a good watchdog, I'll let you stay with your human, Mr. Patch."

Patch barked his appreciation.

"This door is locked and intact," Rebecca said after pushing on the sturdy back door. She turned up the propane-powered lamp to cast away the shadows.

"Denke," Samantha replied, touched at how matter-of-fact Rebecca and Isaac both were, considering the situation. "Patch does keep me calm."

"We have our bedroom here." Rebecca grabbed a flashlight and pointed it down a short hallway to the left. "And here is the kitchen and living room."

She checked the front door and deemed it intact.

Samantha took in the scent of lemon wax and lavender mixed with the country smells of fried chicken and earthy undertones from fresh vegetables.

The house was neat and clean. Smaller

than Micah's and pretty in a minimalist, plain way. "It's lovely, Rebecca," she said.

Rebecca smiled. "This house used to be full of boys. I miss hearing them stomping around at dawn, so it'll be nice to have someone upstairs."

Isaac came in with her small suitcase, while she clung to her tote bag that held her laptop and other things.

"Follow us," Isaac said as he turned to the right of the living room and started upstairs. "There are two rooms and a small bathroom up here."

He moved ahead, turning up the propane lamps in each room and checking the armoires and crannies. "All clear up here."

Samantha knew the bathroom would be functional and that was all she needed. "This will be great," she said, her words dragging.

Isaac left Rebecca to help her settle in. "You come put your clothes in this chest," Rebecca said, her hand on a tall chifforobe. "I'm going to make us some chamomile tea so I'll meet you downstairs."

"Thanks," Samantha said, realizing she'd used English. Old habits went both ways in her case.

Rebecca turned at the door. "We'll do everything we can for you, Samantha. Isaac sleeps with one eye open anyway since we raise chickens and sell the eggs. Predators do come calling."

Leon was a dangerous predator. She only wished she'd seen that before now.

"I know you'll do your best and I'm thankful," Samantha replied. "Why would you want to risk it?"

Rebecca took her hand, her brown eyes full of sincerity. "Martha loves you and that means we do, too. So we protect those we love."

Samantha heard the earnest truth in those words. Nodding, she held in her tears and swallowed.

Rebecca patted her hand. "You can sleep well tonight." Then she turned for the door.

"I'll be down soon," Samantha said, too overcome for much more.

After Rebecca left, Samantha sank down on the bed and stared into the darkness,

Patch by her side. *What should I do, Lord? How can I get out of this?*

Patch nudged her hand with his cold little nose. He knew her fears.

The silence that followed brought her no answers. Tomorrow, she'd continue on the action she'd planned on taking when she arrived. The police knew everything now, at least. She'd go into town and try to reach Dorothea and find out more about Leon's ex-wife. Her assistant could tell her what was going on, she hoped. She had to be careful and explain to Dorothea not to tell anyone where she was. Leon already knew, obviously. She didn't want Dorothea to risk her life to help Samantha.

That would be a hard task. Dorothea loved animals and she loved her job at the clinic. All of that had to change for a while.

Because Samantha couldn't go back there until she knew Leon was behind bars. And maybe not even then.

On her third morning there, Samantha woke early. Not that she'd slept very much.

After dressing in a deep green dress that hit her midcalf, she grabbed her sneakers and tied the white laces. She'd gone into town with Isaac and Rebecca two days ago and she'd recharged her phone and laptop at the Campton Center.

Nathan Craig had met her there and told her he was still trying to find out what he could on Leon Stanton.

"He's clean on paper," Nathan reported. "I've got people going deep into his background. We'll trip him up sooner or later. I'm thinking he has a shell corporation set up to hide the smuggling ring and he probably has several offshore accounts. So far I can't find that information. The authorities are watching for him—just to question him since none of his underlings are talking."

"Did you find anything on the tow truck?"

"Yes," Nathan said. "It was a local from the next town over, about twenty miles from here. Someone paid cash to have the truck removed the morning after the storm. No record of who. The truck driver said he'd left it at a warehouse two counties over. I can't find a trace of it."

"So we only know the wrecking company's name, not who the truck belonged to?"

"Nope. And the license plate was ripped off after the accident. So nothing much there."

"I tried to find out more about his wife," Samantha admitted. "I was afraid to dig too deep. He's probably destroying files and wiping out everything that shows his online footprint."

"You should stay off your computer and your phone," Nathan cautioned. "If he's savvy with electronics, he can easily find you." Giving her a world-weary glance, he said, "Let me work on that angle."

"And what about my friend Dorothea Ramsey?" she asked.

"She seems to have disappeared," Nathan replied. "Your clinic is shut up tight. No animals remaining."

Samantha worried about Dorothea day and night and hoped she had moved what few animals they'd been housing to safe places. While Samantha had been in the private conference room at the center, she'd phoned her friend. Dorothea's phone went straight to voice mail. Afraid to leave a message, Samantha had to give up.

Now, Patch nudged at Samantha as she tied and pinned her apron. She tugged her hair into a passable bun and managed to get the white organdy *kapp* on without a mirror.

"I know. You need a break and some breakfast."

Her face clean and her teeth brushed, she went downstairs. The smell of bacon and fresh coffee greeted her.

Patch barked a woof of appreciation that caused Rebecca to turn around and laugh. "Someone is hungry, ain't so?"

"Good morning," Samantha said. "I need to take him for his morning break before he gets to eat."

Rebecca squinted. "For sure. The yard is available. And Samantha, Isaac is out taking care of the livestock, so be mindful."

So far, no one had bothered her here. She

worried about Micah and the twins. Were they okay? Would he bring them by to visit?

"I will, *denke*," she replied to Rebecca.

The sweet couple had mothered her and chatted with her and shown her how to help around the house. She couldn't ask for a better sanctuary, but she missed seeing the twins playing with Patch and she missed cooking and cleaning the kitchen with Micah.

She especially missed Micah.

What was wrong with her?

Lord, my life is in a mess and I don't know how to get out of it. I could use some guidance.

Samantha longed for a strong cup of that coffee, knowing Patch couldn't wait. She put him on his leash and opened the back door. Standing on the porch, she searched the entire backyard and saw the barn doors thrown open.

The world looked normal. The huge oak tree that shaded the house stood solid and steady. A pleasant summer breeze pushed at her bonnet strings and stirred at her skirt. This Amish uniform wasn't much different from the scrubs and lab coat she'd worn on a daily basis for so long.

Checking the trees along the land break, she was thankful that this farm had very few woods close by. She looked to the east, thinking that small copse of trees would lead to her grandmother's house. That little forest was the only cover all around. Not many places for anyone to hide.

"Go ahead, Patch," she told the furry little dog.

Patch gave her a thankful look, his dark eyes trusting as he scurried in front of her. After he'd sniffed and taken care of business, he lifted his black nose in the air, his nostrils flaring. Then he started barking and tugged at the leash.

He wanted Samantha to follow him to the chicken house behind the barn.

TWELVE

Micah missed her already. How could he have gotten so used to having Samantha in his home?

He missed how she helped with breakfast every morning and insisted on clearing the dishes away at every meal. He missed her good home cooking and how she made the washed clothes seem so much fresher.

"Micah?"

He turned from staring out the window to find Emmie standing there in her muck boots. *"Ja?"*

"The barn door was open," she said, her green eyes shimmering with fear. "I was afraid to go inside."

Micah went into action. "Where is your *bruder*?"

Emmie glanced around. "I don't know. I thought he was with you."

Micah took off toward the barn. "Stay here. Stay inside, Emmie."

"But—"

"Stay here. I mean it."

He was out the door and hurtling toward the barn when he saw Jed coming around from the back. Breathing a sigh of relief, Micah caught up with him.

"What's wrong?" Jed asked, his face bright with sweat, his movements twitching and unsure.

"Emmie couldn't find you," Micah explained. "Have you been in the barn?"

"Not yet," Jed admitted. "I heard a noise out back and I came to see. I was coming to get you to show you."

Micah followed Jed, dread in each step.

"Our hogs got out. I can't find a one of 'em." Jed pointed to the pig corral.

Micah ran to the open gate of the pen that stood out away from the barn. He'd placed it back near the trees for a reason. The pigs he'd bought to purposely raise for meat and to sell at market were now scattered to the wind. He'd have to go into the woods to round them up. Normally, he'd take Jed with him.

He couldn't do that now. This had been deliberate.

Emmie! He'd left her in the house.

"Jed, come with me," he called. "Hurry."

They both took off toward the house.

"Emmie?" Micah's voice echoed through his ears, but it seemed only a whisper to him. He called out again as he rushed inside the house.

Samantha followed Patch inside the small, clean barn. "Isaac?"

She heard a moan coming from the tack room. Patch took off, barking and prancing back to her to make sure she would follow.

Samantha hurled herself inside the tiny room and gasped when she saw Isaac on the floor. "Isaac?"

She dropped down to touch his arm. "What happened?"

Isaac opened his eyes and moaned again.

"Someone hit me over the head," he said, pointing toward the back of the barn. "I tripped him before I went down and he fell against that old wheel lying over near the back door. Got up and ran before I could get to him."

Samantha helped Isaac sit up, then she checked his pulse and his head. "You have a small knot on the back of your head," she said, relief washing through her. "Are you dizzy?"

"*Neh*, not too much," Isaac said, squinting. "I think the man got up and left when he heard Patch barking. That little dog always comes through."

Samantha wanted to run out the back and check, but she needed to get Isaac up to the house. "Can you stand?"

He nodded. "I've been through worse," he said on a chuckle. "This ol' head is hard and stubborn."

She found his hat and shook the grime off. "Let's get that doctored and covered before you put your hat back on."

Slowly, she helped him to his feet and

they walked together out of the barn. When they reached the front, Samantha saw Rebecca standing on the porch.

Fear in her eyes, Rebecca headed toward them. "What's happened?"

Samantha explained as she helped Isaac up to a chair on the porch. "It had to be someone here to scare me."

"I don't know," Isaac said. "Could be those *rumspringa* teens making mischief. The teens I hire to help out now and then never have liked Old Henry."

"Did you see one of them?" Rebecca asked, her tone shouting anger. "Did that ornery bull butt someone?"

"I got a glimpse. They weren't Amish. A man for sure, in different clothes. Still it could have been one of those boys messing with me. I'm surprised Old Henry didn't finish 'em off."

Old Henry was the mean bull he'd mentioned to Samantha when she'd first arrived. They'd also talked about some of the local Amish teens who liked to act out and cause trouble. Samantha figured the people who were after her had tried to harm Isaac so they could sneak to the house and find her.

Rebecca scoffed. "Why would a teenager hit you over the head? Teenagers are reckless, but I've never known them to hit an elder over the head."

Isaac shrugged and winced. "They also might want to steal some equipment to barter for beer and such."

"No matter, right now I'm more concerned with you."

Rebecca fussed over him while he kept pushing her away. "I'll be fine."

Samantha helped him into the house, then sat down and stared at her hands while Rebecca cleaned and bandaged his wound.

"Is he okay?" she asked later, guilt coloring her words.

"He has a hard head," Rebecca replied. "But this is worrisome."

"The man wasn't wearing Amish clothes," Samantha said. "It had to have been someone looking for me."

"It does seem suspicious," Rebecca said. "I never thought they'd find you here."

"I can't keep hiding out," Samantha replied, determined to end this one way or another. "At least not here. They know I'm in this community. I need to leave and this time I'm going to do what I set out to do."

"Honey, don't make any rash decisions," Rebecca said.

Samantha stood and starting pacing. "No, they're doing these things on purpose—to scare me, to frighten the whole community. They could have easily come into your house or Micah's by now and killed me." She stopped and stared out the window, the pretty summer weather making her wish she could be safe and out there living her life. "He wants to antagonize me to come out of hiding, Rebecca."

"Why?" Rebecca asked, her usually serene expression changing into a worried frown.

Samantha held her hands together. "Because he wants me alive," she said. "He wants me alive so he can torment me and make me feel guilty before he kills me."

* * *

"Emmie?"

Micah burst through the back door, calling her name while his imagination created horrific scenes. Jed followed, the door clashing behind them.

Emmie came running out of the mudroom, fear in her voice. "What's wrong?"

Micah ran and lifted her in the air. His heart beat so fast, he had to take a long breath. "I was worried. I left you alone."

She gave him a puzzled stare. "I'm not a baby, you know."

Micah settled her back on the floor and touched a hand to her hair. "No, you're for sure not a baby. We have to be careful these days."

Emmie's gaze moved to the kitchen. "We have a visitor," she said, giving Micah a warning with her eyes. Turning, she said, "Matthew brought a casserole from his mom."

Matthew Kemp stood in the kitchen holding a casserole dish, a dare in his eyes.

"What are you doing here?" Micah asked, his fears becoming real now.

"Gut mariye," Matthew said, a twisted smile on his face. "I called out and Emmie let me in."

Micah wanted to be relieved, but Matthew should have found him before coming inside his house. *"Denke,"* he said, taking the dish. "That was nice of your *mamm*."

Matthew glanced around, his expression dark despite the wry smile. Then he walked around, picking up a dish here or a towel there. "We heard you had a houseguest. An *Englischer*." He snarled that term. The Kemp boys were known for disliking the *Englisch*.

"Our guest has left," Micah said, leaving it at that. He didn't like how Matthew seemed to be snooping about. Was he hoping to make trouble or steal something when no one was looking? Or worse, had someone purposely sent him here?

Placing the dish on the table, Micah motioned to the door. "I'll walk you out, Matthew."

He wondered where the younger brother was. Had Samuel opened the gate to the hog stall? Why would he do that?

Matthew glanced back at the field. "Heard about that explosion the other day. You've got a lot going on lately."

"Yes, we're getting back to normal."

When Matthew realized he wasn't going to get any gossip from Micah, he frowned and lifted a hand. "Got to go. Just wanted to help, if you need me and my *bruder*. We like to make money during first cut and we saw you tilling one of the fields the other day."

Had they been watching his house?

"Denke," Micah said. "I have plenty of help right now. I'll keep that in mind for the second cut."

Matthew's grin went sour. He left in a hurry, getting on his horse and taking off toward the road.

Micah's warning radar went up. This visit seemed too coincidental and contrived. The Kemp boys did come by at times, looking for work or bringing food, but to have Matthew show up this morning, with the hogs out in the woods, didn't seem like an accident.

For now, he'd try to believe that Matthew had truly only been dropping off food. The boys were a handful. However, he didn't think they'd bring harm to his home.

Those ruthless people had to leave him and his family alone. Samantha had come and gone. Did they think he knew something now? They had to have seen the police and firemen here the day of the blast. What if they'd taken Emmie while he was out there with Jed? If they had sent Matthew in to find out information or to present a distraction, this could become even more of a problem than he'd thought.

Fear for his family and for Samantha filled his head.

Sitting both of his siblings down, Micah went over the rules again. "Remember, don't open the door to anyone without me here in the house," he said. "And don't go to any of the outbuildings alone."

"Will it always be this way?" Emmie asked, her tone full of resolve.

"I hope not," Micah replied. How could he be sure?

"That's why Samantha left, so now we're safe," Emmie said. "I wish you'd made her stay."

Jed tried to look stern before Micah caught the fear in his brother's eyes. He had to try to calm both of them.

"I know things have been strange around here since the tornado, but Samantha is not our kind. She belongs in another world and the people harassing her belong there, too. They could harm us. That's why she left. She didn't want to bring us harm."

Emmie scrubbed a hand across her face. "I don't care if she's *Englisch* now, I miss her and Patch."

"I do, too," Micah admitted. "And even though she's staying somewhere else, we still need to keep nearby each other. I was fearful for you, Emmie."

His little sister nodded. "It was only Matthew." Then she whirled. "Oh, I almost forgot. I was sweeping the mudroom and I found something odd on the shelf."

Micah's whole system went on alert. What now? "Show me."

She went into the mudroom and reached up on a shelf, then turned to hand him a small flat black orb not much bigger than a penny. "What is this?"

Micah studied the thin round item. "I have no idea. You found it on the floor?"

"Neh," Emmie said, motioning with her hand. "I was sweeping underneath the washer and looked up and saw it on the shelf by the window. I thought it was a bug, so I hit it with the broom. It fell off the shelf. What do you think it is, Micah?"

"Ah, maybe a washer part I could have placed up there," he replied, pretty sure this didn't belong on the old washing machine.

Micah's pulse bumped into double-speed. Samantha had told him Leon Stanton was a techie—a person who loved all things technological, such as drones, smartphones and...the latest security measures. He didn't know much about technology. Still, he had a bad feeling this little orb was some kind of wireless device.

Possibly a listening device or a tracker of some sort.

Was this why they'd tampered with the mudroom window? They must have lowered this device in through the small opening and tucked it far back on the shelf. The wringer washer would have shimmied and shaken enough to cause this little device to slide loose from its hiding place.

"Thanks, Emmie," he said. "I'll figure out where this goes." He didn't want to scare his sister or alert anyone who might be listening, so he put it back where it had been for now.

He needed to let Samantha know about this. If he was correct, this meant Leon had been listening in on their conversations—in this room for sure and maybe in the kitchen. This would also explain how he knew exactly where she was at all times. It also meant Leon now knew she'd left with Rebecca and Isaac. Micah had to hurry and warn her.

* * *

Micah needed to round up the hogs and pigs, but he now had a more urgent matter to take care of. The hogs might come home since they knew when feeding time happened. He placed a small trough of feed inside the open gate, hoping they'd gather there and stay.

After cleaning himself up, he took the twins to Jeremiah's and waited until they'd run off to play with the other *kinder*. He showed Jeremiah the little device Emmie had found, putting a finger to his lips.

Jeremiah studied it and turned it over in his hand. Motioning to Micah, he took him out to the backyard and placed the device on a garden table.

He walked with Micah away from it and talked in a whisper. "*Ja*, this could certainly be what the *Englisch* call a bug," he explained. "A listening device, for sure." He kept an eye on it while he spoke. "Wireless and probably long-reaching, so they had to pry the window open and push the device to the back of the shelf. Might have used some type of adhesive that broke loose when the wringer was going, or it could have fallen when Emmie hit at it."

Still talking low, he said, "Normally, they'd drill a tiny hole and hide it better. It could stick to any surface and remain out of sight."

"I have to warn Samantha," Micah said. "I'm not sure how long I'll be." He glanced at the porch where the twins laughed with Ava Jane and the Weaver children. Thankfully, the twins were close in age to Sarah Rose and Eli. Little JJ followed them around, his curiosity strong.

"They will be safe with us," Jeremiah reassured him. "We love having them so why don't you let them spend the night. They entertain JJ and they're always willing to help with chores. So take your time and be aware. Oh, and have Samantha check anything she brought with her, too."

"*Denke*, Jeremiah," Micah said. "That's kind of you."

Jeremiah nodded and motioned to the

device. "I will make sure this thing never works again. I have a *gut* sledgehammer."

"He'll know we found it," Micah said. "I don't want it in my house."

"Don't worry about that," Jeremiah replied. "Go after Samantha and keep her safe. I can tell you care about her."

Micah's shock must have registered on his face. "She needs to know this."

Jeremiah gave him a wry smile. "She also needs to know what I can see clearly. You do care about her."

Micah wished he had someone to guide him through this. Jeremiah had always come through and the man had a shrewd sense of knowing things. He was right. Micah wanted to see Samantha and make sure she was all right. He'd have to tell her about everything that had happened today, even if he couldn't prove the people after her were still harassing him. It could have been those rambunctious teens out for more fun.

Either way, he had to warn her about the listening device and warn her that Leon might have planted one in her personal items, too. He prayed he'd get to her before anyone could harm her.

THIRTEEN

Samantha had a plan. She'd wait until dark, then go through the woods to her grand-mother's house. She sounded like Little Red Riding Hood, but she had to stop Leon somehow. She wouldn't put any more inno-cent people in his path. If that storm hadn't hit, she would have gone straight to Gram-ma's house anyway. Her car would be hid-den in the barn and no one would know she was even there. Just for a few days.

Now, things were worse than ever.

Nerves scratching down her spine, she went into the kitchen to help with supper. They'd all stayed close to the house once Isaac and Rebecca had fed the animals and watched the roads and woods. Samantha's skin burned hot, as if crawling with ants.

She had to be away from here. Away from

the fear of someone getting hurt. Away from the threats and the teasing harassment of a madman. No one could find Leon and stop him. He was goading her and the authorities because he knew how to get away with things.

When she heard a buggy jingling up the drive, Samantha hurried to the upstairs window.

Micah!

She hadn't realized how much she missed him until he got out of the buggy and tied up the horses. Where were the twins?

Patch barked a happy bark and scrambled down the stairs like a black-and-white soccer ball. Samantha's heart roiled with Patch.

She tried to calmly make her way down the old, creaking stairs. Stopping at the last steps, she stared down at him. He wore fresh clothes and smelled like scented soap. So he'd cleaned up to come and visit?

"Hello, Samantha," he said, his tone full of both exhaustion and acceptance while his eyes seemed to shine brightly as he watched her. Yet, he was still guarded, hesitant.

"Hi, Micah," she replied. "Where are the twins?"

He glanced from her to Rebecca and Isaac. "They're with Jeremiah and Ava Jane. I... I need to talk to you."

Her pulse beeped inside her ears. Sure that he could hear it and her unsteady shortness of breath, she nodded.

"Go out on the back porch," Rebecca said. "Can you stay for supper?"

"Maybe," he said, looking unsure. "You both should hear this, too."

"What happened?" Samantha said, the hopefulness she'd felt on seeing him now disappearing. Dread and fear filled her heart. "Micah, what's wrong?"

He held to his suspenders. "So much. First someone opened the gate of the pig stall and the hogs got out. Then Matthew Kemp showed up with a covered dish, asking a lot of questions. After he left, Emmie remembered she'd found a strange black button-looking thing in the mudroom."

"What do you mean?" Rebecca asked, hands on her hips.

Samantha closed her eyes. She knew what he was saying. "Leon's men planted something in the mudroom?"

"Planted?" Isaac joined his wife in frowning.

Samantha held to the newel post. "It's a device—a listening device, small and round like a black button. Am I right, Micah?"

He nodded. "Jeremiah confirmed it for me. He's probably destroying it with a hammer as we speak."

"A listening device," Samantha said, feeling violated and abused. "He heard things we've said about…everything."

"I think so," Micah replied. "Which means he knows you're here, too, probably."

Samantha glanced at Isaac. "Someone hit Isaac over the head this morning while he was in the barn. This has to be Leon's work. I've decided he doesn't want to kill me. He wants me back long enough to tell me how I've ruined everything. So he's sending people to frighten and intimidate all of us." She stopped and took in a breath, her eyes downcast. "After he's berated me and made me feel guilty, then he'll get rid of me."

"No one is getting rid of you," Micah said. "I know you well enough to figure you'll try to make a run for it. Tonight maybe?"

He did know her, Samantha thought. "I can't continue to let this happen. The crimes of mischief are a distraction while he finds a way to catch me. As I told Rebecca, he's got people doing his dirty work so he can come at me. And yes, I'm going to do what I'd planned all along. I'm going to my gramma's house and if he shows up, I'll be ready for him."

Micah shook his head "*Neh*, I won't let you do that."

"It's not up to you," she argued. "This is not your fight, not your choice."

"I told you, it became my fight when you landed in my field, Samantha. He's harassing you, me, and now Isaac and Rebecca. If he knows you're there alone, he'll get what he wants. You'll walk into his trap. He has to have done background checks on you and he probably knows from our conversations that you have a relative here and you want to go to her house. It's not a wise decision."

"And staying here is?" she asked, frustration cracking her voice. "He'll kill one of you to get to me."

"I think we need to keep you hidden," Micah said, "but put out the word that you've left or that you're in protective custody. Anything to make him think you've moved on."

"We tried that and it's only been a few days," she argued. "He knows my every move so I'm going to end it by letting him come for me. I'll be ready."

"Ready? How so?" Isaac asked, a frown on his usually calm face.

"I don't know yet. My phone is fully charged. I'll call for help and maybe an officer can hide there with me. They can capture him. If that doesn't work, I'll run."

"And have them ambush you in the woods?" Micah replied.

She shook her head. "I have to get away, somehow. I ran track in college. I can run fast."

"Do you hear yourself?" Micah asked in a gentle tone.

Samantha's gaze locked with his. Why did she feel such a pull toward this person? Maybe because he'd saved her and he'd hidden her in his home? He was a good man and she'd just left a bad man? He wanted to protect her, but she was used to protecting herself. She didn't know how to let anyone help her.

Maybe Leon had seen that independence in her, too, and he'd hoped to break her and remold her into the kind of submissive woman he needed.

"I made a mistake in coming to Campton Creek and now I'm going to remedy that. I'll call a cab or an Uber."

Micah gave Rebecca and Isaac a quick glance. "No, you won't do that either. You and I will wait here until dark and I'll go with you to your *grossmammi*'s house."

Shocked, she shook her head. "No, Micah. That's not proper and you know it. You can't abandon the twins to protect me."

"The twins are safe with Jeremiah and his

family and they can stay the night. I'll only be there with you until dawn. You can call a cab or leave however you want."

"She can continue to stay here," Rebecca pointed out.

"She won't," Micah said, his eyes back on Samantha. "Am I right?"

She nodded. "Yes, I'd planned to leave tonight, one way or another."

"So you won't stay here and let us watch out for you?" Isaac asked.

"I won't stay here because I don't want Leon to harm either of you," she replied. "I'm done running. He's the guilty one, not me." She sank down on a chair. "I want to go to my gramma's home and be alone. I can find my way into town and call a cab. I'll take a bus back to New York and turn myself in to the FBI. They can protect me."

"Because we can't?" Micah asked, hurt and worry in his eyes. "I've watched out for you for almost two weeks now, Saman-tha. You have to know I'd do anything to help you."

"I do know that," she replied. "And that's

the problem. You shouldn't have to be taking care of me."

"Let's have supper and think about our options," Isaac suggested. "It's been a long day and my sore head is hungry."

Micah didn't argue. Samantha went to help with the fried chicken and vegetables. They all sat down and tried to eat. Each time one of them suggested she stay, Samantha shook her head. She'd stalled long enough. She had to go back and face whatever waited in Winter Lake.

As nightfall settled in muted hues of pink and gray, Samantha prepared to leave. When she came downstairs, she looked over to where Micah sat with Isaac while Rebecca moved around the kitchen.

"Micah, you don't have to do this. It's a short distance to Gramma's house. I should be okay."

"I'm walking with you. My buggy isn't moving so they'll think I'm still here. I hope they won't try to find out otherwise."

In the end, she stopped arguing with him. Truth be told, she'd welcome his company.

Micah did make her feel safe. She couldn't let anything happen to him. Emmie and Jed needed him.

She needed him. That wasn't an easy admission and she wasn't sure where that kind of longing could take her. He could never know her feelings. Never.

She'd hold Micah King in her heart for a long time to come. If she could stay alive to do that.

"I'm ready."

Micah turned from staring out into the dark to find Samantha standing with her bags, still wearing the Amish dress she'd had on earlier. She looked Amish, looked as if she belonged here in this community. With him.

He needed to tamp down these feelings that had started surfacing since the day he'd found her. Nothing could come of him pining away for someone who'd chosen the *Englisch* world over his world.

"Let's go then," he replied, walking over to join her. "Are you sure?"

She gave him a nod. "I'll hide there until I can sneak away." She touched his arm. "I'm leaving Patch here. I want you to take him to the twins. He's been through enough."

Micah swallowed the roiling emotions he'd tried so hard to hold at bay. "Emmie and Jed will be glad to watch out for him."

Rebecca hugged Samantha close. "You be extra careful, okay?"

Isaac stood back. "I wish we could do more."

Samantha patted his hand. "You have all done more than enough. I will always remember your kindness."

Now that it was full dark, Micah guided her out the back door, then checked all around the house. "A full moon," he noted. "Not good for us. We'll hurry across the open field and get into the trees."

He watched as Patch tried to follow, watched as Samantha worked hard to hold back tears.

Rebecca held the little dog, gently speaking to Patch to keep him calm.

Micah took Samantha's hand. "I won't let you go into those woods alone."

"Denke," she said, her eyes holding his. "I'm glad for your company."

Micah would always love the way she thanked him. So he held tightly to her hand and wished he didn't have to let go.

They silently set out across the yard, the night damp and full of the scents of jasmine and honeysuckle while the moon cast gray, muted shadows all around.

They made their way through the field, following a path that had been forged over the years. Micah listened for the sound of footfalls, but only heard critters scurrying away and the buzz of mosquitoes near his ears and the cicadas calling all around them.

"You are brave to make this decision," he said on a whisper, only because he was so concerned about her and hoped to talk her out of it. "I know you want to get on with your life."

"And so do you," she replied, her tone low.

"You've been a big disruption but... I

didn't mind so much. I have a routine that gets boring at times."

Her low laughter echoed softly into the night. "Well, the last couple of weeks sure changed that."

They reached the small copse of trees and shrubs that separated the Witmer property from her *grossmammi*'s place.

Micah held her there, his hand on her arm. "Samantha, you have to understand I don't want any harm to come to you."

"I do understand," she said. "You've been good to me, Micah. You've put yourself in harm's way for me. I can't let you continue to do that."

"Or is it you don't want me to continue to help?" he asked. "Maybe you want to go back and confront Leon since you weren't given that chance before."

She gasped and pulled away. "That's ridiculous. I want this over so I can rebuild my life and my practice. I can't live in Winter Lake after this. I'll have to move and start over. I don't want to see Leon Stanton ever again."

She took off into the woods, leaving him there shocked and even more confused. Micah hurried after her, wishing he hadn't blurted that out.

He'd caught up with her when she screamed and backed against him. Two dark shadows loomed in front of them. Someone had been waiting for them in the woods.

FOURTEEN

Samantha screamed again.

One of the men lurched forward and tried to grab her, his face hidden by a dark bandana. Samantha pushed at him and scooted away, watching in horror as Micah tussled with the other man wearing dark clothes and a kerchief over his face.

"Micah?" she called, trying to find a way to help.

Glancing around, she spotted the man she'd pushed away coming toward her. When her foot hit on a rock, Samantha dove for it and came up in time to hit the man over the head.

He moaned and fell to the ground, then started crawling toward her, his beefy hand grabbing at her ankle, then finding her skirt.

She heard a tearing of material but managed to squirm away and stand unsteadily.

"Leave me alone," she screamed as she slipped again and tugged to get up. Her hands scraped across dirt and rocks as she pushed back up.

Micah rolled on the ground, his fists hitting at the man holding him. With a grunt, he managed to throw the man to the side and scrambled up. "Run," he called to her. "Hurry."

"No." Samantha wouldn't leave him. "Not without you."

The injured man stood and weaved his way toward her again.

She searched for another weapon. Through a veil of moonlight, she spotted a broken limb lying on some bramble and tore through the bushes to grab it. Quickly, she lifted it over her head as the man ran toward her, his head down like a bull's. Samantha slammed the sturdy limb with baseball-bat efficiency toward his head.

The impact of the limb hitting his nose cracked through the night. The limb, still fresh from the tornado, held. He moaned again and slumped over, then fell to the ground. Moaning, he rolled away and lay there.

She ran toward Micah as he scrambled to get up. "Micah!"

Micah took the limb from her and when the other man came after him with a roar, he swung toward the man's midsection and missed. Micah brought the sturdy limb up again and rammed it against the man's forehead.

The attacker screamed in pain and fell. Knocked out cold.

Micah rushed to Samantha. "Are you all right?"

She nodded. "We need to get away."

"Wait," Micah said, his breath coming in huffs. "I think I know these two."

"Know them? How?" Samantha held to him as he leaned down to pull one of the bandanas off the man he'd coldcocked.

Micah let out a grunt when he saw the man's face. "This is no man. Just a boy. This is Samuel Kemp, John Kemp's boy. And I'm thinking that one there is his brother Matthew."

Micah held the moaning, confused man while Samantha pulled the bandana away from his bloody face. "He's not any of the guards I know."

"It's Matthew," Micah said, his voice drained and aggravated. Tossing Matthew back to the ground, he stared down at the half-conscious figure. "I should have known they'd have something to do with all of this. Especially since *he* showed up at my house this morning. My guess is they're the ones who keep snooping around the barn and tampering with fences and such."

"But why? Do they have something against you?" Samantha asked.

Micah shook his head. "*Neh*, they have a thing for making money—any way they can."

Samantha's gaze moved between the two men. "Oh, no. Leon got to them. He hired them to harass us?" Gasping, she said, "One of them probably attacked Isaac this morning."

"At about the same time the other one was at my house, asking questions about my *guest.*"

Micah felt sick to his stomach. That someone from his community could be a part of such evil was beyond him. "He must have offered them a lot of money, maybe told them not to kill anyone, which explains why they've gone only so far. We'll find out when they wake up."

"That would mean they were trying to take me alive."

"And at least knock me out, so they could get you away."

"How do they keep finding us?"

Micah shook his head. "These two know all the right questions to ask. By hiring someone within the community, he can find out anything he wants."

Micah checked them for weapons. After finding a knife on Matthew and a small handgun on Samuel, he threw the weapons into the woods in a spot nearby. "I'd tie them up if I had some rope." Tugging at her, he said, "Let's get out of here. They'll come around and you shouldn't be here."

"We have to call for help," she said, pulling out her phone as they hurried through the woods. "At least now, maybe some of this mischief will stop and you can find a little peace."

Once they were a safe distance away and hidden behind some trees, Micah pulled her close, so close she felt as if he'd kiss her. Instead he leaned his forehead against hers and whispered, "With you around, Samantha Herndon, I don't know if I'll ever have any peace."

Samantha saw his wry smile, yet flinched at his words. He could tell he'd hurt her, but what could he say? That he didn't want to lose her?

"I'm calling the police," she said. "Then I'm going home to my gramma's house."

With that, she turned away and dialed 911.

Micah waited for her to finish. Before he could explain his words, she said, "They'll take them in for questioning and throw them in jail for harassment and property damage. I told them I wasn't waiting for them to arrive. I gave the dispatcher their names and this location. I'm not so sure I want the police to know where I'm going tonight, so I didn't mention that."

"I'll handle the police and I can identify the Kemp boys in person tomorrow morning," Micah said. "Right now, let's get you to the house."

"Maybe the police will get here soon." Taking another look at them, she asked, "Why did these two have to get involved?"

"Let's keep moving," he said, taking her arm to guide her out of the thicket and back onto a worn footpath. "There's your *gross-mammi*'s house. Can you see it?"

Samantha looked across the field and saw the white house shimmering a bright gray in the moonlight. "I do see it. At last."

"Let's hurry then." He took her hand, wishing he could make her feel safe. Samantha held tightly to him, her fingers interlaced with his, as they jogged toward the house.

"This is so wrong," she whispered as they ran toward her gramma's house. "You've been so kind to me, Micah, when I've caused you so much trouble."

He stopped when they reached the lane to the house. "Samantha, listen to me," he said, turning to stand in front of her. "Listen."

She looked up at him, her eyes full of an innocence that disputed everything she'd been through, a trust that he didn't deserve, and a longing he wasn't sure he understood.

"Samantha..."

She was listening, but he couldn't find any words. So he got closer and put his hand on the back of her neck to pull her toward him. Then he leaned down and kissed her, the touch of her lips like sweet, warm nectar. The kiss told Micah everything he needed to know. She felt the same. She returned the kiss and pulled back to stare up at him, her eyes glistening in the moonlight.

"You were saying?"

"I should get you inside," he said on a husky whisper.

She nodded and held on to his hand. They went up the short drive and walked around to the back of the tiny house.

"Do you have a key?" he asked, still reeling from their kiss. A kiss he should regret, only not right now.

"I'll see if it's still where she used to hide it." While she searched for the key, Micah stared through a window.

"Samantha," he said, grabbing her as he got in front of her. "Someone is inside."

Samantha held to the key she'd found in a flower pot and watched as a shadow moved through the dark house. Still off-kilter from the kiss she'd shared with Micah, she stood in the warm wind, unsure what to do now. "Who could it be? Not the Kemp brothers. We would have seen them."

"Only one person that I see," Micah replied as he stared through the window. Then he whispered, "I think it's a woman."

"What?" Samantha squinted through the window by the back door. The figure turned, then they heard a scream.

"She needs help," Micah said, trying to open the door. "Give me the key."

Samantha shoved it at him, her heart pumping against her chest so fast she thought she'd pass out. "It might be a trap."

Micah wasn't listening. He got the door open and shoved it hard back against the wall. Samantha rushed past him and lunged at the woman standing in the dark, holding a frying pan. "Who are you?"

The woman screamed again and dropped the pan onto the table before she stepped out of the shadows. "Leah, Leah. It's me. It's Gramma. I screamed because I saw a face at the window."

Samantha dropped her own bags and ran straight into her grandmother's arms. "Gramma, it's so good to see you." Then she burst into tears.

"What's this?" Gramma said, stroking Samantha's head. "Why are you roaming around in the middle of the night to give me a heart attack?" She looked at Micah. "And with such a *gut* dear man at that?"

Micah stepped forward and held a hand

on Samantha's shoulder. "It's *wunderbar gut* to see you, Martha."

"Same here," Martha said. "And not a minute too soon, if you ask me." Her shrewd gaze moved over both of them. "Your clothes are torn and dirty. What have you two been up to?"

"It's not what you might think," Micah said. "Samantha will have to explain since it's not my place." Giving Samantha an apologetic glance, he stayed close as if he still wanted to protect her.

Samantha stood back and wiped her eyes. "I wanted to see you. So many bad things have happened and I made a mess of things and now I'm in danger and everyone is in danger—"

"Now, Micah," Gramma interrupted, "please turn up a lamp and let me get the kettle going. I'm in need of some strong tea."

Micah moved over to the small kitchen. "I'll make the tea, Martha."

Martha took Samantha and sat her down on a blue chair by the small settee where they used to read together. "I came home to see what all was going on," Martha said. "And to see with my own eyes if the letters I received are true. My beautiful *kleindochter* has returned to Campton Creek."

"How did you know?" Samantha asked, too overwhelmed to think straight. "Someone wrote to you?"

"Rebecca wrote to me," Martha said while she patted Samantha's hand. "She said you didn't want to bother me. Once she wrote the whole story I knew I had to return."

"It's too dangerous," Samantha said. "I planned to hide out here, alone."

"Nonsense," Gramma said, clucking like a mother hen. "*Schtobbe* that right now."

Micah brought them tea and sat down across from them. "I tried to tell her to *stop* it. Thought it was a bad idea."

"So did you plan to stay here with her then?" Martha asked on a stern voice, a gentleness in her eyes.

"*Neh*, I planned to get her here safely and leave in the daylight."

Martha looked from Samantha to Micah.

"I see you have a champion here, but it would not do well to be seen here together with no one about."

"That's why I told him he didn't have to watch after me," Samantha replied through a sniffle. "I'm a mess and you know I'm usually strong-minded and independent, Gramma."

"Ach jah," Martha agreed. *Oh, yeah.* "So explain yourselves. And, Leah, start at the beginning so my tired brain can keep up."

Samantha took a deep breath and told her grandmother what had happened. Micah added to the story here and there and soon they had Martha up to date on the whole situation. "I'll have to go to the police station and see what's to happen to the Kemp boys."

"Those two—always up to no good," Martha said on a huff. Giving Samantha a frown, she said. "So you've been roaming around the community, hiding from this man?"

Samantha nodded. "If I could have made it here to your place, I think I would have been safe and no one would have known. The storm changed all of that."

Her gramma looked from Samantha to Micah, her brown eyes bright with hope. "*Er*, maybe *Gott* changed all of that, ain't so?"

An hour ago, Samantha wouldn't have thought about God's hand in this. But now, when she looked at Micah and remembered his lips touching hers, she had to wonder.

Did God have a plan for her life? Every threat she'd avoided, every fear she'd lived through, every emotion she'd experienced in discovering Leon was a dangerous man who'd used her and lied to her, and yet she'd somehow survived. Had all that she'd been through finally brought her home? And would Micah play a role in her future?

FIFTEEN

True to his word, Micah had slept on the small sofa until around four in the morning. Then he'd silently left and found his way back to Isaac's house to take his horse and buggy home. Isaac had put the horse in a stall and left the buggy nearby. He came out of the house just as Micah had harnessed the horse, Patch on his heels.

"So, young Micah, how did it go last night?"

Micah lifted Patch in his arms and told Isaac what had happened. "I hope to talk to Samuel and Matthew today and... I hope to check on Martha and Samantha later."

"So Martha is back and the Kemps are in trouble. Good news and bad news, and so early in the morning at that."

Micah nodded. *"Ja*, and I have the alfalfa first cutting to finish."

"Make hay in daylight," Isaac replied. "Rebecca can check on her friend, Martha. She'll be so glad Martha is back."

"Denke," Micah said, leaving Isaac to go about his work. He had a crew coming to finish the cut, so that would give him time to go into town and get back to help the rest of the day.

Micah went by Jeremiah's place and found his friend doing the early milking. After he explained what had happened, Jeremiah shook his head.

"Those boys have always been trouble. Now they're stepping into criminal territory. Petty crimes so far, but still they could have killed someone." He placed a pail of fresh goat milk on a table in the barn. "Not to mention, this man will probably try to kill them to keep them silent. Are you sure they didn't up and leave? Someone could have been waiting nearby and picked them up. If they had planned to take Samantha, they'd have a vehicle parked close."

Micah nodded. "The police were on their way. We didn't want to wait around in the dark, in case one of them came to. I'm going to the station to talk to them and see what can be done. For now, Samantha is safe with her *grossmammi*."

"We hope," Jeremiah said. "Martha is formidable, but so is your enemy."

An enemy Micah hadn't asked for, one he'd gladly fight to save Samantha. "I'll check on them, don't worry."

Jeremiah touched him on the shoulder. "I'm not worried. I can see in your eyes that you have feelings for this woman."

"What would that matter?" Micah asked. "She is *Englisch*."

"You're asking me?" Jeremiah said with a smile. "I've been in that world, and I came back here. I was accepted and well, you know the rest of my story."

"*Ja*, I do." Micah chuckled. "I don't think Samantha will return to the fold. She seems very much attached to her world."

"She was attached to her work," Jeremiah

replied. "Maybe she could do that same work here."

Micah didn't want to hold out hope on that. He'd never heard of a woman animal doctor. This community could use one. "I have to go," he said. "I'll come around to get the twins as soon as I'm finished."

"They will be fine," Jeremiah said. "I'll put them to hoeing vegetables and digging up potatoes."

Micah left, longing for the old days when vegetables were all he had to worry about. Now he had to worry about his siblings and a woman he was beginning to care for way too much.

When he got to the station, the officer at the desk told him the Kemp brothers were not in jail.

"What do you mean?" he asked, stunned. He really wanted to talk to both of them and find out if they knew where Stanton might be. "Did they need medical assistance?"

"Probably, since we found traces of blood nearby," the desk clerk said. "But we'll never know. When our officers arrived at the location, they didn't find anyone there. Found the gun and knife the caller reported. I'm sorry, son. The two men were gone."

"But they attacked a young woman and me last night. They were both near unconscious when we left."

"We have the details of the call and we came straightaway. The boys weren't anywhere in those woods, Mr. King."

"They must have woken up," Micah said. "I should have stayed there with them."

"And you might have been killed if you had stayed," the officer said. "Look, we've got multiple complaints on those boys before. No one in your community is willing to press charges. This latest is concerning so if you want to give a detailed report on what happened last night and regarding the other peculiar events you've mentioned, we can take care of that."

"I'll give a thorough statement because I have reason to believe the Kemp boys are responsible for the property damage behind my barn and other such nonsense," Micah replied. "I don't have a problem pressing charges."

The officer gave him an understanding nod. "They've moved from harassment and petty theft to attacking people. If we find them, we'll bring them in and we'll need someone to identify them and press charges. Or the DA can go after them, but he's not likely to mess with the Amish unless they mess with our world. Too much on his plate already as it is."

Micah's anger boiled over, but he held it in check. He'd heard those same words when his parents were killed. In the end, the drunk driver had gone to jail, only for a few years. Vehicular manslaughter.

Would Leon Stanton and his cronies manage to go free after all? Or would he let his hired instigators take the fall for his evil ways? The Kemp boys were in over their heads and now they were hiding out. Or had they gone missing? Could Stanton be holding them or hiding them?

Bought and paid for, Micah thought as he left the jail. Did their poor *mamm* even know where her boys were? Leon Stanton had bought their help and now he could be buying their silence. What if they were never found?

He had no choice but to go and get the twins and head back home. Maybe he should go and check on their *mamm*. She'd need friends around her right now. And Samantha would need to be aware they were still out there somewhere.

He wondered what he should do about Samantha and her *grossmammi*. Someone needed to watch over them, too.

He left and hurried his horse toward home. When he passed the huge Bawell place, he had an idea. He'd have to convince Josiah and Raesha first, then he'd have to convince Samantha and her gramma, too. It just might work.

Martha stared at Micah for so long, Samantha wondered if she'd turned him to stone. "You want us to do what?" her grandmother asked, her tone full of disbelief.

It had been a whole day and a half since

she'd seen him, a day where she and Gramma had laughed and cried and prayed together. They'd baked pies and cooked supper and talked well into the night. It felt right, being here in the little country house where she'd always been so safe and secure. She'd still lain awake half the night, listening. She'd opened her laptop long enough to find a little bit of information on Leon's ex-wife. She'd remembered he had lived in Newark, New Jersey, before he came home to live in the family estate. She'd sent word in a note to Nathan, hoping he could come up with something based on that.

Samantha couldn't sit still. She could dig a little as long as her laptop had power.

She'd brought this to her gramma now, so she planned to do something, one way or another.

Micah had shown up today with another idea in mind.

He glanced toward Samantha, uncertainty in his eyes. She gave him her own disbelieving glance. "So you come bursting in here and tell us that we're to move in with the Fishers and Naomi Bawell. We're getting used to being here together."

She remembered Naomi and Raesha Bawell. When she'd lived here with Gramma, they visited each other often and saw each other at church. Gramma used to take Samantha to quilt frolics at the big Bawell home, where several women would gather to eat, gossip and pray while they stitched their beautiful creations.

Raesha had been a young bride the last time Samantha had seen her. She'd heard they'd both become widows, and Raesha had remarried a man named Josiah Fisher. Gramma's letters were always full of news. Samantha had good memories of the times they'd spent together. But staying in their home? Sooner or later, she was going to have to take a stand on her own.

Micah's suggestion was surprising.

"I've talked to Josiah," Micah said, his eyes full of hope now. "Raesha said you are both welcome to come and stay with them. They have lots of space and they're known for taking people in."

"I don't need taking in," Martha protested. "Leah... I mean... Samantha...can go and should. She'll be safe there with so many people coming to visit the hat shop and the trinket store." Turning to Samantha, she said, "You can blend in better."

"I'm not leaving you, Gramma," Samantha replied. While she appreciated seeing Micah again and was thankful for his help, she wished he had discussed this with her before asking Josiah and Raesha Fisher to get involved. "Micah, we're doing okay here so far."

"It's only been a day or so," he reminded her. "I would have come sooner, but I had to work yesterday and I had to talk to Josiah and Raesha. This man who wants to take you back has corrupted two members of our community and you said yourself he won't stop until he has you."

Martha frowned, worry in her eyes. "Do you think this man will find her here?"

"I do," Micah said. "I know he will. So far, he's had her driven off the road, destroyed her vehicle, hired people to harass her and me, and they tried to kidnap her the other night, not to mention he's put my siblings in danger and terrorized the whole countryside."

Stopping for a breath, he went on. "If we don't hide her in the last place he'd suspect, she'll still be in danger. That's why I didn't think she should stay here alone. It would be easy for him to connect her to you. Besides the Kemps probably told him she's here in your home now."

"She's right here, listening," Samantha pointed out. "You know I'm used to making my own decisions, so why can't you trust in that?"

Micah shook his head. "I'm sorry. I know you want to do this on your own to keep everyone safe, but we've gone beyond that. We will shield you, so we need you to trust us. Can you do that?"

Martha gazed at Samantha. "He does have a point. You need to be hidden and hidden well. The Bawell women take in people, so no one would suspect and no one in the community would tell anyway. They're all trying to protect you."

"That's the problem," Samantha said. "Everyone is trying to protect me. I never meant for anyone else to get involved in this. Do I stay here and move from home to home? When will it end?"

"It will end when Leon Stanton is brought to justice," Micah said. "Nathan assures me that some of Leon's cronies are talking now. Since they're behind bars and he's not, they're making deals."

"That gives us hope," Martha said. "But until then—"

"—until then you are still in danger," Micah gently said to Samantha, his gaze holding hers, reminding her of the kiss they'd shared.

"I think we can manage here," she retorted, apprehension making her sound less sure than she wanted to feel.

"How?" Micah questioned. "What if he sends those other men again, who are more dangerous than two kids out for kicks and money?"

Samantha let out a sigh. "I don't know. I don't want you to get hurt, Gramma. What do you think?"

Martha glanced from Samantha to Micah. "There is always safety in numbers. While I'm glad to be back in my own home, I'm not opposed to being around others who can watch after us—until this is over. And here in Campton Creek, we do tend to surround each other with love and strength. Those two combined will be better than you and I sitting here like perfect targets."

Micah's eyes softened. "There you have it. I'm not close enough to protect you and keep an eye on my own place and the twins, too."

Samantha's determined stance went away. "And if I stay here, you'll be torn between doing both and your farm work. I could go back to Winter Lake and talk to the police there. However, my instincts say that's a bad idea."

"I agree," Martha said.

"So do I," Micah pitched in.

"Seems I'm outnumbered on this," Samantha replied, glancing around. "Well, Gramma, we had one whole day and this morning to visit and enjoy the quiet."

"*Gott* willing, we'll have more such days," Martha said. "For sure, it will be nice to visit with Raesha and Naomi. You'll like Josie. She's Josiah's sister and she is now married and lives next to the Bawell place—in the old Fisher house."

Samantha couldn't help her smile. Gramma had always loved frolics and visiting with the community at church or any other event. "Sounds as if we won't get bored."

"*Neh*, and you'll be much safer there," Micah said.

Martha gave Samantha a knowing glance, then looked back at Micah. "And much closer to you, ain't so?"

Samantha met Micah's gaze, but neither of them confirmed what Martha was implying. Not with words, anyway.

SIXTEEN

"I feel like a vagabond," Samantha said a couple of days later. She was dressed Amish in a dark green dress with a white apron. Glad she'd brought her own tennis shoes, she leaned down to tie one of them before she went back to stuffing things in her big tote bag. Now she had dresses mixed in with her jeans and T-shirts.

Gramma chuckled. Samantha could see the strain of worry on her face. "I feel much the same. I'm thankful your aunt Laura has recovered and I'm glad I got to see her and help her in her time of need. It's nice to be home, but I'm concerned about you. My dream would be to see you staying here forever, safe and sound."

Samantha turned from packing to smile at her grandmother. "I have to admit, in spite of the circumstances, it's been good to be back at home."

Gramma's mouth dropped open. "You called this place home. Do you feel that way—that this is truly your home?"

"Yes, I do." Samantha sat down on the bed and held her hands in her lap. "I always felt safe and secure here with you, Gramma. And these last couple days have been so precious. I love my work and I liked living in Winter Lake, and now…now I don't think I can go back there."

Martha sat down beside her and took her hand. "Are you saying you might consider returning to Campton Creek? For *gut*? Could you possibly find contentment here, maybe continue in your animal practice?"

Samantha thought about Micah and Emmie and Jed. She'd loved cooking for them and doing her part around the house. Other than her work, she really hadn't missed a lot of her old life. She worked all day and for the most part, went home to read, watch a little television or study up on the medical journals required for any veterinarian. Dinners with Leon and hanging out at his big estate had been the highlight of her life. Could she leave all of that behind?

Gramma had instilled thrift and humility in her. Leon used to tease her about being so frugal when he wanted to lavish her with gifts. His money had been ill-gained and she was so glad she hadn't accepted all of his gifts. The one lavish gift she had accepted—an engagement ring—had only brought her grief.

"I don't know, Gramma. I'm confused about so many things. I fell for the wrong man and now my life is ruined and he wants to make me suffer. I won't go through that, ever again. I won't make any rash decisions right now. I have to wait until I know Leon is behind bars and out of my life before I can move forward and even practice being a veterinarian again."

"What about Micah?" Gramma asked. "He is a *gut* man and he would willingly take care of you."

"He's great," Samantha admitted. "I don't need a man to take care of me, though. I want a partner who sees me as equal and independent. Leon tried to take care of me and I got used to it too much. I've always been capable of making my own money and living my own life."

"Micah wouldn't change that," Gramma said. "I can tell he respects you. You'd be equal in his eyes, even if our ways are more traditional."

Samantha thought about that. Micah did seem to respect her and since he played the role of parent to his siblings, he'd learned a lot about what a woman's day could involve.

"He also feels responsible for me, but this is not on him. I'm the one who showed up here, scared and confused. I'd be long gone if I had my car. Leon is out there and he's watching, so I feel trapped."

"You're not trapped, you are being sheltered from harm," Gramma replied. "There is a difference." Then she leaned close. "Do you have feelings for Micah?"

Samantha couldn't look her grandmother in the eye. Lowering her head, she said, "I don't know."

Martha lifted Samantha's chin and smiled at her. "I can tell you two care about each other, ain't so?"

Did it show so clearly? Samantha swallowed and measured her response carefully. "I do care about him and the twins. They've been so kind to me and I enjoyed my time with them. It's asking a lot for anything more."

"What if Micah wants more?"

"I don't think he wants anything except for me to be gone. The other night he indicated I'm nothing but trouble."

Gramma laughed again. "Men have a funny way of trying to explain themselves, especially when it comes to love."

Love?

Samantha shook her head. "It's not that. Micah and I are from different worlds. I might not be accepted back here. I don't know if I want to live here. It's too much to comprehend right now."

"Have you talked to him about this?"

"No." Samantha stood and finished packing. "There's no reason to talk to him when it's clear he's as frustrated and afraid for his family as I am. I want my life back, and that won't happen in Winter Lake. It might not happen here. He wants his routine, a simple life, and I'm not a part of that routine. I'm a distraction and I've forced him to put himself in a dangerous situation."

Gramma stood, too. "Maybe when this is over?"

Samantha shook her head. "I can't predict that. I can only hope Leon will mess up and finally get put where he belongs, in a prison cell."

Gramma hugged her close. "We will pray. *Gott* will see us through, no matter."

"I hope so."

Samantha wished her faith could be that strong. Why had she decided to come here of all places? She could have gone straight to the police or even the FBI. The fear of not being taken seriously had scared her out of doing that. Leon knew too many powerful people and he would have turned the tables on her. He'd tracked her here, so he had all the power.

She wanted to take her power back. At least, at the Bawell place she could go to the hat shop and recharge her phone and laptop. She was thankful for that. The more she could dig and compare with what Nathan had found out, the better her chances of surviving this. The police could only do so much.

Gramma pulled her out of her thoughts.

"*Kumm*, let's have some tea while we wait for our ride," Gramma said. "I've got bread and preserves to gift our hosts. And we will do our share of the chores, of course."

Samantha finished up and once again brought her bags and set them by the door. When the kettle whistled, she said, "I only agreed to this because I want to keep you safe. But, Gramma, I'm not moving again. This is the last time. If something else bad happens, I will find a way to leave Campton Creek and I'll find Leon myself. He wants me, so I'll go to him to end this."

"Don't go taking things in your own hands," Gramma warned as she handed Samantha her hot tea. "And don't sacrifice yourself to a madman. Promise me you won't do that."

They sat to have their tea when Samantha's phone buzzed. Surprised and afraid, she grabbed it out of her bag. "Hello?"

"Samantha, it's Nathan Craig. I have news, and it's not good."

"What is it?" Samantha asked as she walked away from her grandmother.

"Based on the information you gave us about Leon living in Newark, we found something on Leon Stanton's ex-wife. Her name was Lisa Proctor before she married him, and she lived in New Jersey. She'd moved out from the city and lived in a house that Leon apparently owned, a secluded little cottage by a lake. It wasn't easy to find any of this. Stanton covers his online footprints like a pro."

"And?"

"I'm sorry, Samantha. She died five years ago—under mysterious circumstances. From what I've gathered, some people believe she was murdered."

Samantha gasped and held her hand to her chest. "How did she die?"

"A car accident. Her car went over a bridge and into a deep ravine. It exploded before anyone could get to her."

"Do you think Leon had a hand in this?"

"I can't say for sure, but yes, I'm thinking probably. The official report says he has an alibi. We both know he could have called the shots. They weren't married at the time of her death, but witnesses say he came around a lot. She'd had a restraining order on him."

Samantha leaned against a table. "I can certainly understand her being afraid of him." Taking in a breath, she asked Nathan if he'd heard any word on Samuel and Matthew Kemp.

"No. I agree with you and Micah, though. After Micah told me what happened, I believe Leon has them with him. He either saved them or…he got rid of them."

When she saw a buggy coming into the yard, Samantha checked to make sure it was Josiah Fisher. "Our ride to my next safe house is here, Nathan. Thank you for finding this out for me."

"I'm trying to locate your assistant. I keep meeting dead ends there. No one is at her house and her car is gone. I asked neighbors, but they said she'd been gone for a couple of weeks."

Almost as long as Samantha had been gone. Did Leon do something to Dorothea, trying to get information about Samantha?

"I'm so worried about Dorothea," Samantha replied. "Something is wrong. She might have fled when she heard the reports. I hope she's hiding out somewhere safe."

"I'll keep you posted."

Samantha ended the call and turned to her grandmother. "The investigator who's trying to help us gave me bad news. I'll explain later."

Martha nodded. "I see Josiah has arrived."

"Yes. Time to lock up and move on again," Samantha said. She took a sip of her tea, then washed up the teacups and sat them on the counter. "I'm so glad you're with me, Gramma."

"I'm glad we're together, too," Martha replied, taking her hand. "This will end, Leah. If you keep the faith and know God won't leave us alone."

Samantha nodded at that. She'd prayed for a way out. She was supposed to trust that God would provide. Meantime, she would stay diligent in finding the truth. Each memory brought out something else to use against Leon. Why hadn't she seen this before?

Lost in her thoughts, Samantha didn't see the other man with Josiah. When she looked and found Micah standing there holding Patch, she almost cried. So like him to want to see her grandmother and Samantha safely to another location.

"Hi," she said, her voice weak with a roiling torment.

"Hi," he replied. "We thought two would be better than one. The roads are treacherous these days." Then he shrugged. "Patch wanted to see you."

She took the little dog and held him close

while he tried to lick her face. "I've missed you, Patch."

"I'll ride with Josiah," Gramma insisted, smiling at the tall, nice-looking man who'd come to fetch them.

Josiah nodded to Samantha and grinned at Martha.

"You should ride in the back with me, Gramma," Samantha said, returning Josiah's nod.

Gramma spryly got on the front seat of the buggy. "Nonsense. Get in before someone sees us," she replied in the tone she used when Samantha was growing up. *"Redd up!"*

Samantha reluctantly got in the covered back with Micah, Patch still yelping lightly at her. She wasn't ready, no matter what Gramma had said. She sent Micah what she hoped was a covert glance. His gaze caught hers and held her there.

"Denke," she said, "for coming with Josiah."

"I had ulterior motives," he admitted. "I really wanted to see you again."

She smiled at that. "Are you getting used to seeing me dressed Amish?"

"I *could* get used to that, *ja*."

The buggy bumped, scaring them both back into the real world. Micah automatically reached over to give her a brief touch on the arm.

"Sorry about that," Josiah said. "The storm left a lot of deep potholes in the road."

Micah kept looking over at Samantha. "I think you'll be safe with Josiah and his family. We've rounded up some people to watch the place around the clock."

"Was that necessary?"

"We want you and Martha to be safe, so *ja*, it's necessary."

Samantha listened while Gramma chattered away with Josiah as if she didn't have a care in the world. Then she told Micah, "I don't know how I can ever repay all of you."

Micah took her hand. "I'm not worried about being repaid. I only want to keep you alive and well." He leaned in. "So maybe I can kiss you again one day."

Samantha wanted that day to come, but

what would come after? Could she have a life here in this plain community, with this man? As they turned into the sprawling Bawell place, she wondered what her life *would* be like if she came home for good.

She also wondered if she'd live to see that day and be able to make that decision.

SEVENTEEN

"We have plenty of room," Naomi Bawell kept telling them from her wheelchair in the corner. "I live in the *grossmammi haus* alone now that Josie has married Tobias. They live across the way in what used to be the Fisher house. You will meet them later when Josie comes over to help with the *kinder*."

The older woman stopped and looked longingly out the window. "I miss my Josie. She tries to come over every day to visit with me. So you see, you're doing us a favor. Martha can visit with me now and you'll be safe here."

"I plan to help out as much as possible," Samantha replied. "This house is amazing."

"And always needing to be cleaned," Raesha Fisher said with her quiet smile. "But we do love it."

Samantha absorbed all of the chatter about her, thanked Josiah and Raesha over and over, and helped clean up their iced tea and cookies after they'd sat and chatted for a while.

After they'd discussed how they'd help her blend in and that people would be watching and reporting on anyone who tried to get near the house, she walked out to the breezeway between the big house and the smaller one where Gramma would stay with Grammi Naomi. Glad that Gramma rolled with the punches, she could tell the two women were close. This might be good for Gramma, at least. She got lonely on her own, same as Naomi.

Overwhelmed, Samantha decided she needed some air to let this all settle in. She wasn't used to the kindness of others and she sure wasn't used to being a nomad.

The peace of this valley helped to calm her. Micah being here also helped with that. He'd left the twins with Rebecca and Isaac. They were like grandparents to Emmie and Jed.

A sweet little family all alone. When she pictured herself staying here, those three always came to mind.

For now, the Bawell house was her temporary home. She had to admit, this place was like a fortress. Off the road, with a storefront hat shop that brought in tourists year-round. While the hat shop was apart from the main house, it was also busy enough to keep away intruders.

She hoped.

Samantha had a room on the second floor of the main house, down the hallway from Josiah and Raesha's room, with a nice view of the creek and the main bridge across it off in the distance. Micah lived closer to the Bawell house. Why that mattered, she didn't want to delve into too much. It did matter. He mattered. Knowing he was across the fields and valleys gave her courage to fight harder against the forces trying to destroy her. Whether she stayed here or not might depend on her job, but it would also depend on Micah.

She could admit that while she stood here alone in the late afternoon breeze with the fragrance of honeysuckles and roses floating through the air.

The door to the main house opened and Micah came to stand with her, a glass of lemonade in his hand. "I thought you might be thirsty."

She took the lemonade and smiled over at him. "I feel so strange these days. Discombobulated."

"Is that a word?" he asked, his eyes sparkling. For a moment he looked young and carefree and it made her heart open a little wider.

"It is a word. It means I feel out of sorts and confused, not to mention terrified."

Micah looked off in the distance. "Josie lives over there in a house that haunted her for years. The man she married came all the way from Kentucky to find her and marry her. She was confused and terrified and now she's a happy newlywed. The house went from being a bad memory to being a new joy."

Samantha glanced over at the property directly to the east of this house. A nice, flower-filled yard and a neat house with a wraparound porch. A big swing hung in one corner of the porch. "I'm happy for Josie and Tobias. My gramma told me some of their story. What are you saying, Micah?"

"I don't know," he admitted. "Except to tell you not to give up. There is always hope."

"I only hope to bring Leon to justice," she replied. "Nathan called me this morning before you came to pick us up. He found out Leon's ex-wife died five years ago." She gave Micah the details, then shook her head. "I think he had her killed."

Micah's expression held shock, his dark eyebrows lifting in astonishment. "But how?"

"He has the means to do anything he wants," Samantha said. "He obviously has ways of finding anyone he wants, too."

"You need to stay off your phone and laptop," Micah said. "If he put a bug in my house, he might be tracing your every move with your devices, too. Jeremiah told me it's easy to do that these days with the smartphones."

"I've tried to stay offline," Samantha replied. "Other than doing research to prove what I saw, I also want to talk to Dorothea. It's not like her to ignore my calls. She has to be scared."

"You can use one of the computers at the Campton Center," Micah replied. "And they have secure phones, too."

"I can't stand sitting and waiting." Samantha took a sip of the tart lemonade. She couldn't eat or drink much these days. "You're right. I'll disguise myself and try to get there tomorrow."

"I will drive you."

"Micah, you have so much to do. You don't need to escort me all over the county."

"I will take you," he said again. "I will work early in the morning and I'll pick you up as soon as I get the main chores done. If you want?"

"I appreciate that," she said, thinking he was the kindest man she'd ever met. "How about you drop me off and I'll catch a ride back. I hear Jewel loves to cart around Amish people in her little car."

Jewel worked at the Campton Center, which was a wonderful resource for the Amish that included pro bono legal advice from Nathan's wife, Alisha, doctors and nurses who checked on the ill, and help with anything as needed. Tobias Mast, Josie's husband, had stayed there when he first came here. Samantha had also met Bettye Willis and Judy Campton, the two matriarchs who held reign over the center and lived in the carriage house.

"Jewel loves life," he said with a smile. "She's close to all of us and she used to be a bouncer in a bar, so she can protect you."

Surprised at that, Samantha stared out into the gloaming. "I'm used to taking care of myself. My mother would pass out on the couch and I'd cook and clean, hoping to impress her.

"She never even noticed. She'd start

drinking early and be out cold by the time I got home from school."

Micah's eyes held sympathy. "Your gramma did the right thing, raising you here."

"Gramma is the best. She never judges."

"Does she…question you about…me?"

Samantha didn't know how to answer that. "She has asked, yes. I told her we're friends and you've been kind to me."

His hurt expression changed to one of resolve. "I should remember that instead of thinking about kissing you."

They stood gazing at each other when the door opened and Gramma walked out, her hands on her hips as she stared them down. "There you two are. Supper is ready."

Micah moved away and let Samantha take the lead. When they passed Gramma, she gave them a knowing smile.

"See? No judgment," Samantha whispered.

When they got inside the humor left her completely.

"We've received word that the Kemp boys have been found," Josiah told them.

His wife Raesha came down the stairs. "Nathan called the phone I use for the shop. We have one here inside the house now since we have the *kinder* to consider when I'm constantly going back and forth from here to the shop."

"Where did they find them?" Samantha asked, afraid to hear the answer.

"Just outside the town proper, near the foothills of Green Mountain," Josiah said. "Samuel has been beaten very badly and… Matthew is dead."

Samantha gasped and grabbed her grandmother's hand. "Do they know who did this?"

Josiah glanced at Micah. "Not yet, but Nathan said they are considering Micah as a suspect."

Micah put his hands on his hips. "What?"

Josiah rubbed his bearded chin. "Nathan said he'd discuss it with both of you when he gets home tomorrow. He's going to investigate further."

Samantha looked at Micah. "Your fingerprints would be on the gun and the knife."

"*Ja,* because I threw them both in the bushes, and we told the police that."

"Leon will say you beat them up, tried to kill them and dumped them over the state line."

"That's not true," Gramma said, indignation in her tone.

"No, it's not true. Leon is only out for himself and he'll lie and blame anyone else to get what he wants," Samantha said. "You should hide out, too, Micah. Or leave for a while."

"I'm not doing either of those things," Micah replied, his eyes dark with an anger that scared Samantha. "We didn't hurt those boys that badly and we were protecting ourselves. If Samuel recovers, he'll tell the truth."

"Not if Leon gets to him first," she replied. "He'll either bully Samuel with threats so he'll be forced to lie or...he'll finish killing him and blame it on you."

"Has anyone checked on their *mamm*?" Gramma asked.

"The police told me they'd check on her," Micah said. "I could go by there on my way home."

"I pray Nettie is all right. She tends to keep to herself and let the boys run their small farm. That is when they aren't in trouble. Matthew's death will take its toll on her."

Raesha nodded at Micah. "She'll need us. Micah, let me know what you find out. We can call on her tomorrow and get people to stay with her and help with bringing Matthew's body home."

"I should go before it gets too late," he said. "I'll let Rebecca and Isaac know what's happened. They can check on Nettie, too."

After he declined supper, Samantha walked him to the door. "Be careful. The police will be watching us even more now. Now they think we did something wrong."

"Me," he said, his head down. "They think I'm a suspect. What will happen if I get taken to jail?"

"I won't let them do that," she said. "You did nothing wrong and you were protecting me."

He gave her a look that told her so many things. She saw concern and remorse, hope and doubt, and she saw a longing that reflected that in her own soul.

"We'll get through this," he said. "We won't let this evil win out."

Samantha wanted to hug him tight and hold on, but she knew the rules. So she stood with her fists clenched tightly against her legs. "I will see you tomorrow, unless you hear any news tonight."

He nodded and walked away, his broad shoulders slumped. To possibly be accused of murder would do any man in, but it would especially destroy this man. He wasn't the kind to bring harm to anyone. And this was her fault.

She had to do something to end this harassment. For this whole community and especially the man she was falling for.

Micah went to Nettie Kemp's place before going to pick up the twins. They didn't need to be here for this. His brother and sister had been through a lot, so he hoped to shelter them from the worst of these criminal activities.

He pulled up to the old house, thinking it looked desolate and in need of some tender loving care. Nettie Kemp wasn't a pleasant woman, even when neighbors tried to be kind to her. The boys hadn't had a *gut* life. No one, however, should have to tell a mother that her son was dead.

Should he wait on that? But then, she'd hear it later and hate him. If he was charged for this murder, she'd really hate him. He had no way of proving he was innocent. Just his word and Samantha's word. Would that be enough?

Micah knocked on the door and waited. He heard shuffling and a woman's voice. Finally Nettie opened the door a few inches. "Who is it?"

"Micah," he said, his nerves on alert. The warm wind picked up and hit against his skin like a warning. The countryside seemed still and waiting. "It's Micah King. I came by to see how you're doing."

"I'm fine. Boys ain't here. Run off somewhere again."

"Can I come in?" Micah asked, wishing he could do more.

"I'll come out."

Nettie opened the door and came out onto the porch. She had aged well past her forty-two years. Her hair held patches of gray and her skin looked shriveled.

"Are you all right?" Micah asked as he guided her to a chair.

Nettie settled and pulled an old shawl around her shoulders. "I've been sick for a while now."

"You cooked me some food a few days ago. I wanted to thank you."

Nettie gave him a confused look. "I haven't cooked in months, Micah."

He should have known the food her son had brought had been cooked by someone else. Just another ploy so they could snoop and find Samantha.

"I must have gotten confused," he replied. "I get food from well-meaning people all the time."

"I do, too," she said, her smile weak. "The boys buy it from all around. *Gut* neighbors check on me and bring so much food, we have to pass some on."

Micah was about to tell her what he'd heard about her boys. When he saw a police car pulling up, the words stuck in his throat. The car parked in front of the house. When the officer got out and saw him sitting there with Nettie Kemp, the frown on the man's face turned to a determined scowl. Micah knew right then he was about to be arrested.

EIGHTEEN

"What?"

Samantha stared at Nathan, not wanting to absorb what he'd told her.

"Micah is in jail," he said again. "They arrested him last night at Nettie Kemp's house."

"No, that can't be." Samantha sank down on the nearest chair, the pounding of her pulse making her dizzy. "We heard he might be a suspect. He didn't do anything except protect me. We used a rock and a limb to fight them both off. Then we ran away."

Nathan glanced from Samantha to her grandmother. Raesha and Naomi were listening. They'd been quilting together. "Captain Schroder found a gun and a knife in the woods. The weapons will be sent to the state lab for fingerprints. They'll take Micah's to compare."

Samantha felt a chill moving down her spine. "He threw those weapons out of reach, then he told the police where to find them."

Nathan nodded. "He did everything right, but his DNA could be on their clothes. Based on Samuel's statement, Micah is being charged for Matthew's death." Holding up his hand, he added, "They really don't have enough evidence, plus Micah is sure to have a good alibi."

"He does," Martha said. "He stayed at my house all night, out of concern for our safety. He slept on the downstairs couch."

"And that was well past the time we called for help," Samantha added.

"That might work toward reasonable doubt," Nathan said. "The prosecution would argue that he had ample time to sneak out and move the boys."

"With a horse and buggy?" Naomi said, scoffing.

"I don't have a horse and buggy," Gramma

said. "I call for taxis or rely on neighbors to get around."

"They could say he arranged for someone to help him," Nathan countered.

"I need to see him," Samantha said, refusing to picture Micah sitting in a courtroom. "I'll explain to Captain Schroder. I was there. They know Leon's been after me."

"Okay, I'll take you to him," Nathan said. "As I explained, the case is weak, but the locals want this over so they're grabbing at any possibilities. You being an eyewitness won't sway them. They think you and Micah have a thing going on."

"A thing?" Gramma looked confused, then shut her mouth. "Oh."

Naomi and Raesha shot Samantha sympathetic glances. "We'd heard you two were growing close," Naomi said. "That doesn't mean you'd murder someone." She looked at Nathan. "Micah wouldn't do that. I believe Samantha and I believe Micah."

"We all do," Nathan replied. "I'm going to talk to people and figure this out, I promise." He nodded to the other ladies. "Alisha is going to counsel him and go before a judge to secure his bail. He's not a flight risk so maybe he'll be home soon. They have motive—he knows the Kemp boys have been harassing him and he had an opportunity in the woods the other night. That coupled with the possibility of his DNA matching, adds up, but he'd have to have had access to some sort of vehicle since your grandmother doesn't have a horse and buggy, and he has an alibi for that night— he spent the night on Martha's couch. Also, he has dependents and a farm that needs his attention. He's innocent until proven guilty and I'm sure Alisha will argue that point."

"He's innocent, period." Samantha wanted to scream. "And as for the rest, Micah and I are close, just a friendship. We both know the rules. I'm telling the truth about what happened the other night. They were after us. After me. They've been harassing Micah and me since…since I arrived at his house."

Gramma took her hand. "Don't worry

about that right now. Do what you must to get Micah out of there."

"Where are the twins?" Raesha asked.

"Rebecca and Isaac have them," Nathan said. "I went by there first. They're asking to come here and see Samantha."

"I'll go and get them," Raesha said. "We will watch after them until Samantha returns, hopefully with Micah. I'm sure they're confused and upset."

Samantha ran for her purse and put her phone and laptop inside. She'd need both later and she didn't care if Leon tracked her down. She wouldn't put Micah or this community through any more trouble.

Micah sat in the jail cell, worry causing his foot to tap nervously against the cold, concrete floor. Humiliated and angry after a night of tossing on the uncomfortable mattress, he thought about Nettie's face when the officer had told her one of her sons was dead and the other at a hospital miles away, fighting to stay alive. When the officer had arrested Micah right there in front of the frail woman, Micah tried to explain. Nettie only heard he'd possibly murdered her son and beat up the other one. The poor woman had crumbled right there on the porch.

Micah had begged the officer to get her some help. Reluctantly, the man had called an ambulance.

Now, cold and tired, Micah thought back over the last few weeks and all that had brought him here. When he thought of Samantha, he felt no resentment. She hadn't brought this on him. Leon Stanton had caused this and Leon had somehow managed to convince the authorities that Micah was a murderer. Micah wouldn't put it past Captain Schroder to take a bribe.

When he heard the door to the two cells opening, he stood and grabbed the bars, hoping someone would tell him his brother and sister were both okay.

Alisha Craig came in with Samantha.

Micah's blush of shame made his skin burn, but he couldn't take his eyes away from Samantha.

Samantha rushed to the bars, her expression full of shock and resolve. "Micah, I'm so sorry."

"The twins?" he asked, trying to hide his surprise at seeing her. He should have known she'd be the first one to defend him.

"They're at the Bawell house, safe and sound. Rebecca and Isaac are there waiting to hear, too. Everyone we love is there."

Everyone we love.

The air went still, and the musty, aged smell of his cell went away. He took in the fresh scent of her hair and skin. Swallowing, he nodded. *"Denke* for letting me know."

Alisha stepped forward, her expression and tone all business, even if she did have an understanding expression on her face. "Micah, we'll get you out of here. These charges are trumped up since the local police department wants to blame someone for all the happenings around here. I'm working on getting you out on bail."

Samantha watched his face, her eyes misty. "Someone called in an anonymous tip saying you did this," she said. "A woman."

"A woman?" That didn't make any sense. "So we don't know who?" He looked from her to Alisha. "Not Nettie?"

"No, I'm guessing Leon paid someone to do it," she said. "He did this and we're going to prove it."

Alisha studied her phone, then glanced at Micah. "We can prove you had no means of transportation to take two fully grown men miles away from where you left them and dump them to die. And…you have a solid alibi. Witnesses who can vouch you were taking Samantha to her grandmother's house and you planned to stand guard until the next morning."

"Which he did. He slept on the couch and Gramma knows that," Samantha added. "I can vouch for that, too. They might think we're covering for you. But even if you left on foot and they think you called a cab, the cab records will show you didn't do that."

"We'll go before the judge later today," Alisha said. "I'll argue that this is a very weak case and they could find your DNA on the weapons and some of their clothes, because you fought in self-defense with the boys. You also called for help and we have the conversation with the dispatcher to prove that. Then you left them semi-unconscious to get Samantha to safety. Also, when we hear from the medical examiner, I'm sure he or she will tell us the time of death as well as the cause and how long Matthew had been dead or if he died on the spot. That should be near the same time you were asleep in Martha's house. You'll be out of here soon, Micah."

"I hope that is the truth," he said, too weary to add anything. "I have to protect my family."

Alisha nodded. "I'll leave you two to visit. You only have a few minutes."

Micah watched the lawyer walk away, her summer dress and light sweater a sharp contrast to her all-business attitude.

"Micah?" Samantha stood staring at him. "Can you ever forgive me?"

Micah reached out for her hand. "This

is not your fault. I understand you blame yourself, but fate had other ideas, Samantha Herndon."

"Fate dealt you a hard blow on my behalf."

"I didn't kill anyone and as long as you know that, I'll be all right."

"I do know that. We all know that."

"The twins?"

"We told them you had to come to see the police, to clear up some things."

"They'll hear. Nettie was in a bad way when I left her."

"I'm so sorry. Rebecca and Isaac were going to check on her and try to assure her you didn't do this."

Micah was glad to hear that. "We have to trust in *Gott*," he said. "We must."

The word would spread and people might shun him. He hoped the people who counted would support him.

"I do trust in Him," Samantha said. "When I leave here, I'm going to the Campton Center to use a secure phone so I can call around and try to find Dorothea. Then

I'm going to work hard to prove you couldn't have done this."

Micah held her hand. "Don't go out on your own, okay? Let justice work, let *Gott* do His work."

"I'm going to try, Micah." She stared into his eyes, unable to speak, but he could see it there in her expression, in the way she held to his hand. "Having faith doesn't mean I have to sit still and do nothing. Not when I'm capable of ending this, somehow. You're too kind and decent to have this happening to you."

"I could say the same for you," he replied, his voice caught up in emotion.

He could see what he knew in his heart. They were falling into a forbidden love. And where would that get them?

He'd have to be the one to push her away so that she could focus on what she had to do. "Go and take care of yourself," he finally said. "I'll be okay."

Samantha's expression deepened into a look of regret, the pain of his brisk brush-off showing in her pretty eyes. "I'll be back. I promise."

He nodded and backed away from the bars holding him. After she left, he let out a breath. She might come back to help him and reassure him, but she'd have to leave soon.

Would he be the same man after she went back to her world?

Samantha sat in the Campton Center with her head in her hands. Frustration burned through her nerves like a hot wire. She couldn't reach Dorothea. She'd called most of their friends and all she'd found out was that Leon was on the run and Dorothea had been hiding out since the clinic shut down. No one back in Winter Lake really knew what was going on. Some of their friends thought Leon had killed both Samantha and Dorothea. Some couldn't believe Leon was behind all of this. They thought he'd been framed. Samantha didn't say where she was—only that they'd had an argument and she'd needed some time away. The rumors were flying. People would assume what they wanted to assume. She knew the truth.

Samantha figured one day she'd be on one of those true-crime shows telling the world she had no clue the man she'd fallen for had been a horrible criminal.

Exhausted, she sat there praying for anything, some sort of break that would give them some relief. She wanted Micah out from behind bars. He didn't belong there.

When the door opened and Jeremiah walked in, she was surprised to see him instead of Nathan or Alisha. "What's wrong?"

"Nothing," he said. The man towered over her and held an air of confidence that made her feel like things would be okay. "I wanted you to know the *kinder* are at the Bawell house, safe and occupied enough that they aren't asking too many questions."

"That's a relief. Maybe Micah will be with them soon."

"We pray." He looked out the window. "Some of us finished cutting and drying his early hay, so he can rest assured on that."

"Denke."

"And, Samantha, I did some footwork on my own. I found out the Kemp boys were being paid by two men who followed them the night of the storm. The boys bragged to some buddies and I was able to persuade those buddies to talk to me."

Samantha didn't want to dwell on how he'd persuaded them. "So they told you the truth?"

"They said Samuel and Matthew were laughing and joking about how easy it would be to get you away from everyone so you'd go back where you belong. They truly thought you had run away from your boyfriend and that you were using Micah to hide out."

Samuel and Matthew had seen her car in the field. How could that equate to her using Micah? "Someone convinced them of that?"

"Ja." He gave her a solemn stare, his blue eyes like a dark sky. "I convinced them otherwise."

She stood. *"Denke.* If this is ever over—"

Before she could promise she'd do her best to pay everyone back somehow, the front door of the center opened and she glanced up to find Micah standing at the door of the conference room.

"Micah!" She rushed past Jeremiah to hug Micah close, not caring who saw. "Micah, I'm so glad to see you."

He held her for a brief moment and tugged out of her embrace.

Backing up, she looked into his eyes and saw hesitation and regret. "Alisha got me out on bail. I don't know who paid—"

"Don't worry about that," Alisha said. "We're going to sit down with Captain Schroder and go over every detail of this case, from the beginning when Samantha was almost pushed off the road, then the tornado and all of the incidents that have happened to both of you since. We'll make a strong case, especially since Jeremiah has talked to people who can testify that the Kemp boys were working for Leon Stanton." She took a breath and tucked back a curl of burnished blond hair. "I'm going to question Samuel again and also remind the captain that he never followed through on reporting back to us about the towed truck or anything else for that matter. That truck held a lot of evidence that's gone now."

"I'm doing everything I can to make that case," Samantha said, glancing at Micah. "I'm so glad you're free."

Micah took a glimpse at Alisha, then turned to look Samantha directly in the eye. "I'm not free until my name is cleared."

Samantha saw the pain and torment in his eyes. He also looked exhausted, that angry frown she'd first noticed when they'd met now back.

Could she blame him after everything he'd been through on her behalf? He'd been gentle with her earlier only to seem so distant now. Had the man she was falling in love with finally had enough of her and all the problems she'd brought with her?

NINETEEN

Three days later, church was being held at the Bawell house, since it was one of the largest properties in the valley.

Samantha checked her *kapp* and hair, using a compact mirror from her purse. She knew the Amish frowned on mirrors, but she had to blend in with all the other women today. She'd been well protected here, mostly staying inside the house with Josie as her companion while they watched after Josiah and Raesha's children, little Dinah and her toddler brother Daniel. She'd met Tobias, Josie's husband. They seemed so in love with each other.

Samantha had to admit, she'd enjoyed helping with the little ones. That made her miss Emmie and Jed, but for now she had to be content with hiding out here.

They could sit on the back porch which was hidden between the main house and the *grossmammi haus* where Naomi and Gramma were enjoying each other's company. They all gathered there most afternoons to sew and chatter while Josie tended to the herb garden and plucked weeds out of the flower bed. Tobias worked part-time at the furniture mart in town and he grew vegetables for several of the local restaurants. Occasionally, he'd show up with flowers for Josie, a smile on his face.

Today, the air was warm and the buzz of bees could be heard near the blossoming daisies and geraniums. She felt almost content, knowing she'd be surrounded by the whole community. Josiah and Jeremiah had agreed she would be hard to find mixed in with the other women who were dressed almost like her. Church. A solid stand against evil.

Now she wore a new dress provided by Raesha. It was blue and Josie had commented on how it brought out Samantha's blue eyes. Her apron was a fresh white and she wore her dependable navy lace-up sneakers. She looked Amish and she had to admit, she wanted to look nice for Micah.

Not sure what was going on in her heart, she only knew that she cared about Micah and the twins. A lot more than she wanted to admit. That might be a one-sided feeling.

He'd been avoiding her since he'd gotten home from jail on Thursday. The last time they'd spoken had been after Alisha had sat with them and Captain Schroder, going back over everything in detail to see if they could connect the dots regarding Leon Stanton.

While the wiry police captain didn't seem to trust anyone, he had listened to Alisha Craig. After she'd shown him the destroyed listening device Emmie had found in the mudroom, she presented a strong case against Leon and the unfortunate Kemp boys. And now they had names of witnesses to back up their claims that Leon had paid the Kemps a lot of money to "scare" Samantha out of hiding. They were waiting for Samuel to recover before anyone could question him, so she strongly urged the chief to put a guard on him. "He's not telling the truth. Someone else tried to beat him to death."

"I can't find my assistant Dorothea," Samantha reminded him. "I've checked with everyone we know. They say she's missing. No one knows where she is."

"I appreciate all of you coming in today," Captain Schroder said after Alisha had finished. "Micah, I'm sorry we had to arrest you, but you were our number one suspect. Even though we've verified most everything Samantha has told us, the Winter Lake police department isn't cooperating with anybody, including the FBI. They've stalled out on all of us regarding Leon Stanton's whereabouts. So I don't have enough evidence to tie him to all of this, but we're getting there." Looking at Samantha, he said, "I'll keep trying to find your assistant, I promise."

"Leon has them in his pocket," Samantha had said. "I can see that now. He's paying them to keep information to themselves.

They've probably been on his payroll all along."

"I'm beginning to see that, too." Captain Schroder played with his ink pen, his shrewd gaze moving around the room. "I'll go and talk to Nettie, tell her I believe you're innocent, Micah. We have enough to at least consider Leon as a strong suspect. And yes, we need to protect Samuel so he doesn't meet the same fate as his brother."

Micah didn't speak for a moment. He gave Samantha a quick, complicated frown. "Well, I'm not in Leon's pocket. And I will do what I have to do to end this. You deserve that much, at least."

Was that a pledge to her, or a release?

But would it stand? Would Micah forgive her? Would her life ever go back to being normal?

Church, even a different kind of church, would seem almost normal. She'd become a backslider in Winter Lake since Leon only went to church to impress people and chastised her when she tried to talk about her faith.

Here, her faith had been challenged and

renewed. This community took care of its own. Jeremiah had returned and become an important part of this town. Josiah had found his sister Josie and married Raesha, and Josie had been reunited with her family and her fiancé, Tobias. They all had happy, settled lives now. Although they weren't Amish, Alisha and Nathan had ties to Campton Creek through her grandmother and his Amish family.

This community truly followed the rules of the *Ordnung* by forgiving each other and showing grace. No matter what.

She could make this work—staying here near Gramma, doing the work she loved on a scaled-down basis. Being near Micah.

Today, she had to think about all of it, surrounded by the whole Amish community. Church would do her good and shield her in a ring of protection. She'd certainly do her amount of praying, too.

Now if she could just see Micah and the twins. Patch missed them since he'd come back here with her. The little dog rarely left her side.

"You have to stay here," she told her furry friend as he tapped his paws toward her. "And stay quiet, too. After everyone leaves, I'll let you visit with Emmie and Jed, okay?"

Patch whined and went back to his bed. He'd been fed and he'd had a long break outside. Church usually lasted hours so he'd be ready to play with the children later.

She shut the door and headed downstairs to help in the kitchen, the pleasant scents of baked casseroles and fresh fruit pies wafting out over the air. The women had brought after-church food—sandwiches and side dishes, easy food to eat out underneath the towering oaks.

When they went outside to find their benches across from the men, Samantha sat with Josie and searched for Micah. She'd already seen Emmie and Jed and got hugs from them.

"You're looking for him, aren't you?" Josie whispered, her brown eyes holding a mature, knowing light.

"Who?" Samantha said, a coy smile on her face.

"You know who—Micah," Josie whispered. "We all think it's so romantic, this forbidden crush you both have on each other."

Samantha shook her head. "It can be nothing more than a crush on my part."

"Well, crush or no, there he is," Josie said with a nudge.

She spotted him in the crowd of men who'd already lined up and taken their seats. He looked like Micah, fresh, his hair curling everywhere, and frowning. But he seemed to sense her there. He turned his head and their eyes met. He nodded and looked away.

He didn't want her in his life anymore.

She sat through the hymns sung in the old language and thought about her life. Samantha made a decision while she listened to the ministers.

She'd find a way to get to Leon. He wouldn't kill her outright. If she could somehow flush him out maybe she could pretend that she cared, that she'd only run away because she was confused. Maybe he'd confess to her. She'd wear a wire if she had to, to prove he was evil.

Then she could be free and clear to make any decisions about her future. After the service was over and they'd eaten, she let Patch out to play with some of the lingering children.

Maybe her future could at least hold Micah and his children as her friends, if nothing else. That would be more than she'd ever dreamed.

Micah finished his meal and threw his trash in a bin that had been set up near the tables. He'd stayed to help load the wagon that carted the church benches and tables around to different locations. He planned to stay later so he could talk to Samantha. He wanted to tell her that he understood she'd have to return to her world and he hoped she'd understand why he couldn't ask her to stay here in his world. He hoped they could stay in touch. He had a feeling she'd visit her gramma a lot now. That might have to be enough—that he'd see her on the occasional holiday or weekend visit.

He'd placed a bench into one of the wagons when Jeremiah rushed up. "*Gut* thing we stationed people on the road," he said, pointing to the end of the winding lane up to the big house. "We have company."

Micah hopped out of the wagon and stared down the lane. A black truck sat parked underneath some trees across from the turn-in. "That's mighty bold of them to sit right there."

"They're waiting as people leave," Jeremiah replied. "Checking all of the women, I imagine."

Micah looked toward the house. "We need to warn Samantha."

"I'll go," Jeremiah said. "You warn the others who are still here."

Micah took off, reporting to several able-bodied men. Then he turned toward the house to make sure Samantha was safe. He was greeted by about two dozen women, all merging together near where they'd been clearing away food. He couldn't even find Samantha in the crowd.

Relieved to know she was being protected, he hurried toward the road with a bold frustration roaring like a thunderstorm through his system. When Josiah tried to stop him, he pushed on. "I'm going to confront them."

"Micah, *neh*."

Micah was beyond caring. He stalked across the old road and went up to the truck, surprising the two burly men inside.

"You've done enough damage here," he said, eying both of them. "I know you have weapons. If you shoot me right in front of all of these people, at least someone will know who you are. You're murderers. You killed an innocent man and beat up his brother, left them both to die. You're finished here, because we're watching you. You can tell your leader that from me. Tell him to leave us in peace. Now leave before the authorities arrive."

By the time he'd finished, several Amish men had come to the road to stand behind him, some of them holding pitchforks and baseball bats.

The men in the truck looked at each other, then back to him. One of them raised a handgun and held it close to his black shirt. "We need to talk to her," he said. "We won't hurt her and we won't make trouble. We need to take her back."

"She's not going anywhere with you two," Micah said, stabbing his finger in the driver's face. "Nowhere. Now get out of here and don't come back. We're watching."

The men gave him an evil glare but cranked the truck and pulled away. Micah let out a breath and turned to face his friends. Josiah and Isaac came to stand with him.

Isaac patted him on the back. "*Kumm* now. You did the right thing. Foolish, *ja*, but the right thing. You always do, Micah."

Micah gathered himself and started back toward the house. Yes, he always tried to do right. This went beyond doing his duty. He cared about Samantha. Too much. She might blend in today, and soon she'd go back to the way things were before.

He saw Samantha moving through the crowd of women to stand apart and wait for him. Did he stop now and talk to her or did he keep away as he'd tried to do over the last few days?

He walked up to her and nodded curtly, then kept going on by. That effort had been much harder than facing down those evil men.

"Micah?" she called after him.

He kept walking until he'd made it to his buggy. He had to find the twins and leave now. Before he did something he'd regret later, like grab her and hold her tight.

When he saw Jed running toward him, he called out. "Go get your sister. It's time to go home."

Jed kept running. "I can't find her, Micah. Emmie is gone. She went to find Patch." He grabbed Micah's shirt, his eyes full of tears. "And now she's gone."

TWENTY

"What do you mean, gone?" Micah asked as he dropped the harness he'd been holding and started moving around the vast yard. "Emmie? Emmie, where are you?"

Samantha came running. "What's wrong?"

"Emmie's gone," Jed said, rushing to Samantha. "She went after Patch and the woman told her she knew where Patch was."

"What woman?" Micah asked as he scoured the countryside, a gut-cutting dread stabbing at his heart. "I don't see her. Which way did they go, Jed? Who was the woman?"

Jed pushed at his hat. "I didn't know her. She said she knew Martha."

Jeremiah and Isaac walked toward them. "What's going on, Micah?" Jeremiah asked.

"Emmie is missing," Samantha replied, giving Micah another scared glance. "And Patch. He ran around the corner. She went to get him."

"Which way?" Jeremiah asked.

"The woman took her into the woods," Jed explained, pointing to the west.

"What did the woman look like?" Micah asked, his heart pumping too fast, his mind going to places he didn't want to think about.

"She was Amish," Jed replied. "I thought Emmie knew her. She looked a lot like Samantha and she said she was a friend of Martha's."

Samantha shook her head. "Gramma would have mentioned a friend. I'm sure she would have introduced me to any friends I don't already know. I didn't see anyone out here. Emmie was playing near the corner of the shop and Patch was right there with her."

"Patch went around the corner," Jed said. "Then the woman showed up and laughed and talked to Emmie. They were going to find Patch in the woods." Jed gave Micah a pleading stare. "I let her go 'cause the woman seemed so friendly. I shouldn't have done that."

Micah hugged his brother and put his hands on Jed's shoulders. "You did nothing wrong. Nothing."

Samantha shot Micah a terrified glance. "I'll go get my phone and call for help."

Jeremiah shouted to everyone to start looking. "She went into the woods," he explained as people came closer. "With a woman dressed as Amish. We think Emmie went to search for Patch."

He motioned for everyone to spread out and soon Micah had a whole team of people calling and searching for Emmie. He tried not to think of her with a stranger. She'd be afraid. She'd be worried about Patch. He wouldn't think beyond that.

When Samantha returned and started toward the woods, he caught up with her. "How could this happen? We've been so careful all week."

Samantha pushed at her falling hair.

"Those two men were another distraction. I should have been watching more closely. I'm sure they timed it perfectly."

Micah didn't respond. What could he say? He'd been out there trying to be the hero with those criminals when Emmie was being lured away from them. If anything happened to her it would be on his shoulders.

Samantha gave him a stare full of pain and regret, but he couldn't comfort her right now. Together, they searched around the shop and the side yard, then hurried toward the trees, following the men who were already forming a grid.

As they entered a copse of trees near the road, Micah heard a dog barking. "Patch."

He and Samantha ran to the edge of the woods, near the road. Patch started barking even louder and jumping in excitement. The little dog was tethered to a sapling, an old rope holding him two feet away from the tree. A food bowl sat nearby.

Jed ran up. "Patch. You found Patch. Where's Emmie?"

That was the question. Micah watched as Jed and Samantha untied the little dog. Watched while his heart shivered in rage and fear.

Where had they taken his little sister?

They'd searched the woods and the creek, hoping Emmie might have tried to get away and could be hiding out near the water. She was nowhere to be found.

Samantha glanced at the sky. A storm was rolling in and it would be dark in an hour or so. No one wanted to give up, so they'd returned to the yard to discuss what to do next.

Captain Schroder came walking toward her and Micah, shaking his head. "I'm sorry I didn't believe all of this at first. We have tried to watch out for this community. I have patrols going around knocking on doors and I've called the state police to ask for help. Some of the sheriff's deputies are willing to help on their own time, too. And we'll put out an Amber Alert."

"Denke," Micah said, his voice raw and

hollow, his eyes rimmed with fatigue and shock.

After the captain went back to the search, Samantha held Micah's arm. "You need to rest."

He pulled away, his eyes on the growing clouds. When he looked back at her, Samantha could see the rage and apprehension threatening to overtake him. He blamed her and why wouldn't he?

Leaning close, he said, "I can't rest. Emmie is out there. She could be alone and afraid or worse, they could hurt her. You know these people. You know what *he's* capable of. So I can't rest until my sister is safe. Please don't suggest that to me again."

Samantha backed away, tears burning at her eyes, her heart so shattered she didn't think she'd ever recover. And if Micah didn't find his sister safe and alive, he'd never recover either. She watched him walk away and turned to go help with sandwiches for the men, her heart heavy with grief and guilt.

Gramma came up to her and took Samantha into her arms. "They will find her. *Gott* has a plan for Emmie."

"Then why did He let them do this to a child?" Samantha asked, rage burning through her. "Why, Gramma?"

Gramma tugged her close again. "We can't question. We can only pray."

Samantha could do that, but would God hear her hollow, weak prayers? She still had her phone in the fold of her apron near her stomach. She knew what she had to do. She'd call Leon and tell him to come and get her. He had to get Emmie safely home first. He'd have to do a swap and let Emmie go. She knew he had Micah's sister, but Samantha would take Emmie's place in a heartbeat. She had to—what other choice could there be? She had to wonder, who was the woman who'd helped him?

When her phone rang before she could even reach for it, she quickly tugged it out from between her apron and her dress. Would Leon dare call her?

The call wasn't from Leon. When she saw Dorothea's name on the caller ID, her heart jumped and became deflated all over again. "Hello," she said, her nerves sending a current of fear throughout her system.

"Samantha, I'm so glad I caught you. I've been so worried."

"Where are you, Dorothea? I've been worried, too. Why haven't you returned my calls? Leon is a dangerous man. You have to hide from him. He kidnapped a little girl today to get to me."

"I know," Dorothea said, her voice low. "He has me. He's been holding me since you left. He's a madman and he won't stop until you talk to him. If you want to see the girl alive, you have to sneak to the end of the road and look for his bodyguards. They'll bring you to him."

Samantha took off running toward the road. "He has Emmie? Is she okay? Why would he do that? Why did he take you right away?"

"Because he thought I'd tell him where you are. He wouldn't let me go. I've been with him for days," Dorothea said. "Hurry,

Samantha. He's threatening to kill both of us if you don't come."

The line went dead.

Samantha tried to absorb what Dorothea had told her. She'd been with Leon this whole time? Why hadn't he used Dorothea as a way to get to Samantha? A sick wave of fear roiled through her stomach. Jed had said the woman looked like Samantha.

Dorothea was older and her hair was shorter, but they both had the same color hair and were about the same size.

Had Dorothea been forced to trick Emmie into going with her? Dorothea could have easily called Patch and offered him a treat. He had always loved Dorothea's treats.

That had to be it. Dorothea had taken Emmie—another evil Leon had forced on an innocent person.

Samantha took off running, tears streaming down her face. When she saw the black truck creeping toward her, she waved the driver down. Just as she was about to get in, she heard Patch barking.

Then she heard Micah screaming at her.

"*Neh*, Samantha, don't do this. Let me go. I'll go with them instead."

Samantha gave him one last long glance as he ran toward her, then got in the truck with the two men. She couldn't look back or hide the angry tears that fell down her face. She had to do this for Micah and the twins.

She'd prayed for a way to make this end. Now it would, one way or another. She had to find Dorothea and Emmie.

Nathan and Alisha came. Micah explained what had happened. He was numb with the kind of pain that he remembered after his parents had been killed. He couldn't lose Emmie, not this way. And he didn't want to lose Samantha—not to that madman who'd been after her for close to a month now.

"Did she take her phone?" Nathan asked. "We might be able to track her if they don't know she had it on her."

Micah had seen her take it out of her apron. Putting his hands against his stomach, he said, "She had it tucked in front, between her dress and her apron where the sash ties, to keep it from falling out."

"That's good," Nathan said. "Let's tell Captain Schroder."

"He took off after them, but we haven't heard from him," Martha said. "What can we do, Nathan?"

"You all need to stay here, in case Emmie might come back. That's a long shot. Stanton obviously has her somewhere nearby. She's smart. She might escape on her own."

Martha touched Nathan's arm. "What about Samantha?"

"She's smart, too," Nathan said. "She'll do what she can to help Emmie." He gave Micah a calm, serious glance. "You know she got into that truck to keep them from doing harm to Emmie. Stanton bided his time and went for something that would make Samantha cave—he took someone she cared about."

Nathan went to his truck where he had a laptop connected to his Wi-Fi. When he returned, he looked grim. "I got through to the captain. He doesn't have the equipment to track a phone to the nearest tower. Even if Samantha has it and it's on, we can't find her."

Jed ran up. "Take Patch. He's been restless and whining. I think he can track her with his nose." When they looked skeptical, he went on. "That's how she found the bad place. Patch took her to it."

Micah didn't even ask how Jed knew that. His siblings had a way of hearing adults talking. Maybe that would turn out to work in their favor this time.

"You're right," Micah said, because he knew Jed felt as guilty as he did about this.

"It wouldn't hurt to try," Nathan said. "We can call for more help, but we'd have to wait."

"Let's go now," Micah said. "They can catch up."

"I'm ready," Jed said, looking taller than he had a couple of hours ago.

"*Neh*, you stay here," Micah replied. "I don't want you to get in trouble, too."

Jed looked disappointed, but he stood back.

Nathan gathered Jeremiah, Josiah, Tobias and Micah. After a brief discussion with Rebecca, Isaac agreed to stay with the women.

"*Kumm*, Patch," Micah said. "Show us where they took Emmie."

The little dog wasted no time taking them toward the woods. Patch turned in a different direction from where they'd been searching.

"He's taking us over the bridge," Micah said as the men followed behind. They moved through the trees, staying silent. Patch seemed to understand. He only stopped to sniff the ground and the air.

Micah figured the woman had stayed on foot, thinking no one would notice and Emmie wouldn't be afraid of searching. He tried to block out the pain of knowing his sister had been taken away and was now in the hands of a horrible, demented man.

Dear Gott, *please help me find both of them. I love Emmie and I love Samantha. I know that's wrong, but I love her.*

It seemed they'd walked for hours when it had only been about an hour. Nathan stopped and held up a hand, then pointed to a rickety old barn at the edge of the foothills of Green Mountain.

The five men hovered behind some scrub bush and rocks, the lush green of the forest hiding them. Patch stood trembling, a low growl emitting from his fierce mouth.

When Micah heard footsteps behind them, he turned to find Jed hiding about ten feet away. Jed saw him and belly-crawled closer.

"I had to *kumm*, Micah. I have to help get Emmie and Samantha back, please?"

Micah tugged Jed close. "Don't do anything foolish."

Jed nodded, his green eyes misty. He must have been following them the whole time.

Patch turned and spotted Jed, then rushed to his side and danced around, but he kept his yelps low. The dog wanted to charge inside. They had to plan this out and make it work. Or they could lose both of the people they held dear.

TWENTY-ONE

Samantha sat with Emmie in a dark corner of the old barn, their hands tied to a post, their feet tied together at the ankles. The scents of brittle hay and damp earth mingled with the woodsy smell of green trees and a hint of rain to come.

Off in the distance, lightning sparked through the sky, followed by a clap of thunder that shook the ground.

Still numb at seeing Leon again, Samantha closed her eyes and fought to gather her courage. He'd been waiting when the truck had pulled up. He'd "escorted" her into what looked like a falling-down tack room and shoved her on the floor. She'd glanced up to find Emmie shivering in a corner, dirt and tears covering her sweet face.

"Get over there with her," Leon said. The

face she'd once remembered as handsome and caring had now become full of rage and resolve, his gold-brown hair tousled and unkempt. His blue eyes held an icy chill while he twisted her arms behind her in a painful, deliberate way. "Miss me much?"

Samantha glared at him but refused to show her fear.

"It will be all right," she kept telling Emmie. "I won't let him hurt you. They'll find us."

"No, they won't find you," Leon said, his face so close she saw the danger in his eyes. "We'll be leaving together soon."

Leon tried to reach for her face when someone called him from the other corner of the barn. Irritation radiated like heat waves off his face. "I'll be right back, darling."

"I didn't find Patch," Emmie blurted after he'd stalked away. "I had to find him. That woman told me she'd seen him in the woods, so we kept walking and walking. I could hear him barking."

"They tricked you," Samantha said.

"We're going to get out of here." She tried to twist the ropes around her wrists. "Keep working on your ties, Emmie. Stop if the door opens and once you're free, pretend you're still tied. I'll get us out of here. Okay?"

Emmie nodded, her fingers working frantically on the old rope.

The door opened about a second after Samantha had given that last warning. Leon walked in, Dorothea with him. Why wasn't she tied up, too?

Samantha looked her over. Dorothea only gave her a twisted smile. "Surprise."

"Are you girls having fun?" Leon asked, his tone full of disdain. "A reunion between friends? Almost as touching as watching you bond with the Plain folks."

"Leon, let Emmie go," Samantha said, hoping he'd listen to reason. "I'm here now and…she has no part of this. She's a child."

Leon leaned over them, causing Emmie to scoot closer to Samantha. "I've heard a lot of your conversations, sweetheart. You and that Amish man laughing and talking, you walking around with the wash in your arms, hanging clothes like a maid."

"You wouldn't understand," she said, a hiss in her words. "You only know how to bully people, deal in stolen goods and...destroy innocent human beings. And you've killed two people, maybe three if we add your former wife."

She looked from his angry frown to Dorothea's tight, smug smile. "Did you know about this, Dorothea? Is that why you're still alive?"

Dorothea walked up to Leon. "I think it's time we tell her. I mean, she won't be around to do any damage this time, right?"

Leon laughed and pulled Dorothea close. "I guess you're right, honey. I think I got the smarter blonde, after all." Giving Samantha a glance that told her he'd be happy to end it all, he said, "Dorothea is one of my top sellers. She moves the fancy designer purses and jewelry. And makes a nice sum of money."

Samantha felt sick to her stomach. Her best friend, the assistant she'd counted on and trusted, had betrayed her in the worst kind of way. "You two deserve each other," she said. "Do what you want with me, but please let Emmie go."

Leon pushed Dorothea away. "If I let the kid go, will you come back to me?" he asked, his voice now silky and smooth.

Dorothea gasped. "Leon, what are you doing? You can't be serious?"

"I'll go with you," Samantha said. "First, you have to send Emmie back to her family. That's the only way."

"Deal," Leon said, moving toward her. "Now that wasn't so hard, was it? We could have done this much sooner if the whole Amish community had minded their own business and stayed out of this."

Samantha breathed a sigh of relief. Once Emmie got away, she'd manage until help came or she'd die trying.

Dorothea blocked Leon, her eyes wild with anger, her blond hair loose and flying around her face. "You can't do that. You said your feelings for her weren't real. You said you loved me."

Leon glanced from Dorothea to Samantha. "You're the one who isn't being real," he said. "I only used you to get closer to Samantha. She's the real prize. Or at least she was." He grabbed Dorothea again. "Now, I'll have to kill you. Then I can leave the country and finally start over. With Samantha."

"Two guards," Jeremiah said after crawling back to their hiding place. "Stanton and the woman are inside. I saw Samantha and Emmie. They're alive and tied up."

Micah swallowed his relief. He still had to get them away from Stanton.

"How do we get past the guards?" Tobias asked.

Nathan pulled out a handgun. "This might help."

Jeremiah shook his head, a calm restraint in his eyes. "I'll take care of them. When I start toward the cabin, all of you except Jed need to rush toward the doors. Don't worry about me and don't stop. Get in, get your loved ones, and get out. Nathan can cover you. Jed, you keep Patch with you."

Micah nodded, knowing he could trust his friend. "So we charge him while you single-handedly take those guards?"

Jeremiah nodded. "*Ja*, with all the might you can muster. And while you're doing that, Samantha and Emmie will do their part to escape."

"How can you be sure?" Micah asked, needing assurance.

"They are together and they are smart," Jeremiah said. "Trust them and, Micah, trust me."

Micah took a deep breath and nodded. "*Ja.*"

While Leon and Dorothea argued and paced, Samantha and Emmie went to work on getting each other free. After straining and tugging at the frayed ropes, Samantha felt hers give. Next, she helped Emmie finish getting her hands loose.

Motioning to Emmie, she scooted around so she could hide Emmie while the girl managed to get her feet free. Keeping her eyes on Leon, Samantha loosened the rope around her tennis shoes. She was free and so was Emmie.

Whispering to Emmie, she said, "When I tell you to run, you do it. I'll say *run* and you go and don't look back, okay?"

Tears brimmed in Emmie's eyes. "I don't want to leave you."

"I'll be okay," Samantha said through the pain in her throat. "I promise," she whispered. "Scoot toward that door over there."

Emmie looked to the left. "I see it."

"Okay, when I say *run*, you run to that door as fast as you can. If you get lost, stay hidden and wait for help."

Emmie sniffed. "I'll get help. Patch will find us."

Leon roared at Dorothea. "I have given you so many opportunities. You came to me, remember?"

"Because you flirted with me and told me you were going to dump Miss High-and-Mighty," Dorothea replied, her skin mottled with red and her eyes desperate and wild.

"If you don't take care of them now, we'll never be free, Leon."

Leon ran a hand over his spiked hair. "I'm not going to kill her, Dorothea. I want to take her with me."

"Over my dead body."

He grabbed Dorothea by the throat. "That can easily be arranged."

"Now, Emmie," Samantha screamed. "Run!"

Emmie hopped up and took off, her hands pushing the old door open. It banged against the outside wall, jarring Leon away from Dorothea.

He immediately went to Samantha and lifted her in the air, his fingers digging into her arms. "What have you done? You're not going anywhere."

"Maybe not," she said, each word full of rage. "Emmie is free and that's all that matters now."

Leon held her close. "I'll never let you go."

Dorothea stood staring at them, a rusty

pitchfork raised over her head. "If you don't kill her, Leon, I will."

Jeremiah gave the all clear and went after the two guards. He grabbed one from behind and had him down before the other one noticed. When the man swung around, Jeremiah knocked him out cold and tossed him against the other one. Then he disabled their weapons and tossed them in the bushes.

Micah and the others rushed toward the rickety double doors at the front of the barn. Patch barked sharply and squirmed in Jed's arms.

They heard shouting from inside and another door on the far side of the barn burst open. Jeremiah whirled to see Emmie running out. She saw him and ran into his arms. Jeremiah held her close. "You're okay. You're okay. Where is Samantha?"

Micah heard her sobs. "Inside. They have her."

Jed ran up to Jeremiah. "Go. I'll watch out for my sister."

Jeremiah gave the boy a pat on the arm and took off toward the others.

Micah hit the doors hard. The old wood splintered as he rushed in, the others behind him. Nathan had his weapon drawn.

"Samantha?" Micah called. A woman with blond hair lay still on the floor, her eyes open and staring up, blood pouring from her chest.

"Samantha?" he cried, rushing toward the woman.

"Samantha is right here."

Micah pivoted as the other men came inside behind him.

Leon Stanton now had a bloody knife aimed for Samantha's heart. "You're too late. We were just on our way out."

Samantha stared at Micah, her blue eyes full of unshed tears. She held her gaze on him as if he were a lifeline.

Nathan held up his gun. "No."

"Put that down or I'll kill her right here," Leon said, his eyes wild and glassy as he inched the knife closer. "I have to take her with me. She ruined my life so she has to pay. I'll make her pay—away from all of you." He shot an angry glare at Micah. "She will always belong to me."

Micah stepped forward, but Jeremiah held him. "I won't let you take her," Micah said to Leon.

Leon scoffed and held Samantha tight. "You can't keep her from me. You tried and you failed. Even the two Amish boys I hired failed me. I had to take care of them, too."

Nathan lowered the gun to the floor and held his hands up. "I think we should at least discuss how this is gonna play out. Samuel Kemp is still alive and he's talking now. Understand?"

Leon snorted. "Nice try." He moved toward the door, parting the crowd. Jeremiah shot Micah a warning look, but Micah was beyond being careful. He looked into Samantha's eyes and knew he'd walk through fire to save her.

Before he could make a move they heard barking followed by a canine snarl. Patch leaped through the open doors and jumped toward Leon's leg, sinking his little teeth in deep.

Leon screamed and tried to pry his leg away. That gave Micah just enough time to grab Samantha and lift her out of Leon's grasp while Nathan grabbed the knife and Josiah knocked Leon to the ground.

Jeremiah put his booted foot on Leon's back then lifted him up, holding him against the wall. "Do not think of moving," he said on a low, confident note.

Patch held on, his brown eyes triumphant, his growls daring anyone to make him stop.

Micah held Samantha in his arms. "It's over," he whispered. "It's finally over."

Samantha clung tightly to him, her eyes full of relief. "Emmie?"

"She's with Jed," Jeremiah said, his arm bearing down on Leon's upper back. "We need to get in touch with Captain Schroder." He reached down and found Leon's phone. "You won't mind if I borrow this, right?"

Leon grunted and glared. "Get this dog off me."

No one obliged him.

Micah lifted Samantha up and carried her out of the barn.

Jed and Emmie ran toward them. "Micah, you saved her!" Emmie shouted.

He gently sat Samantha down on a jutting rock, then gathered his brother and sister close. "We're all safe now."

A gentle rain started to fall. Emmie and Jed danced, holding their heads up to the sky.

While Micah stared into Samantha's eyes and wondered if she'd leave him now.

Two days later...

"Why hasn't she *kumm* to see us, Micah?" Emmie said for the tenth time. "I miss her and Patch. Patch is a hero, you know. He helped get Samantha back."

Micah stopped tinkering with a harness and went to where his sister sat on a blanket by the open door, holding a baby goat. "I told you and Jed, Samantha has a life and it can't involve us."

"But she likes it here," Emmie said. "She

could stay with us. You could marry her. The bishop likes her."

Micah had thought of nothing else the last two days. He'd marry Samantha in a heartbeat, if she'd have him. What did he have to offer her? She'd have to accept this life.

Jed came running out to the barn. "We have company." He waited, then reached out his hand. "It's Samantha."

Emmie squealed, scaring the tiny goat. When they heard a loud, happy bark, she squealed even more. The goat went running into the barn.

Micah stepped out and stared at Samantha. She had on a long floral dress and her hair was up in a bun. Patch jumped and yelped until Emmie and Jed took him to play.

Micah couldn't move. "So you're leaving?"

She nodded, her hands twisting together. "Yes. I have to go back to give my statement and…put my clinic up for sale." Glancing out at the field, she said, "I'll have to return to New York for the trial but that might be a while."

"Where will you go?" he asked, knowing the answer wouldn't be near him.

She hesitated, looking out toward the field. "I thought I might come back here to Campton Creek."

"Ja?" He moved closer, praying, wishing. "To stay?"

She nodded again. "I can get a license to practice in Pennsylvania."

"So you'd live nearby?"

She moved closer. "I'll be staying with my gramma for a while."

"Are you coming home, Samantha Herndon?" he asked, his heart opening wide with hope.

"Do you want me here, Micah King?" she replied, tears in her eyes.

"I could use a *gut* animal doctor, *ja.*"

"If the bishop approves." She moved closer, the scent of a thousand flowers surrounding her.

"Oh, he'll approve. He has five fine horses that always need attention."

"And what about you? Do you approve?"

He pulled her into his arms. "I do. I want you with me for the rest of my days."

"Is that a proposal?"

"Is that an answer?"

"Yes," she whispered. "Yes."

"Yes," he responded, his forehead tucked against hers. "Yes."

He kissed her. Patch starting barking, Emmie squealed again and Jed stood there, grinning. The baby goat made a run for it.

Fall...

"The wedding was beautiful," Gramma told Samantha as she kissed her and hugged her tight. "We are so blessed to have you back, Leah Samantha."

Samantha looked across the yard at Micah. He stood in his black church suit, smiling as he talked to his friends. Isaac, Jeremiah, Josiah, Tobias and Nathan all stood with him.

She glanced around at her new friends. Raesha and Josie had been in charge of the flowers. Ava Jane and Rebecca had helped with the wedding cake and making Samantha's pretty light blue dress. Gramma and Naomi had helped with all of it. Jewel, who'd insisted on being the wedding coordinator, had brought Judy Campton and Bettye Willis to enjoy the festivities. Alisha had offered to help Samantha get licensed and settled into a new practice. With the money she'd gotten after selling her Winter Lake clinic, Samantha would build a small animal hospital out back and she'd travel as needed to the area farms.

A perfect day in a special place.

Micah came up to her and held her close. "I'm so glad you landed in my field."

She laughed and thought about the horror of the summer. Leon would be in jail for a long time, his operation shut down and done. His estate was up for sale. She pitied him, but she had to forgive him, because this had happened. This day.

"I'm home," she said to everyone who'd gathered around.

Jeremiah tugged Ava Jane close. "We're all home."

"Let's eat cake," Jed suggested.

Patch barked at that idea.

The sunset hung smiling to the West over the creek, making it sparkle like gold. Samantha had come here to be saved, and that is exactly what had happened.

* * * * *

Dear Reader,

This is the last book of my Amish Seasons five-book series. I fell in love with the small community of Campton Creek, PA. And I have Jeremiah Weaver to thank for that. He came into my head on a day when I was doubting my storytelling abilities. I felt his torment and saw his story. That book was *Their Amish Reunion*. Since then, I've created many characters who return to Campton Creek to find love and faith again.

All of the books are set there, but they all stand alone plot-wise. These characters spoke to me and showed me the way.

In this last book (for now), and once again, the characters showed me the way in writing this emotional story. I wanted to end this phase of the series with returning characters who all come together to help Micah, the Amish man who falls for Samantha Herndon, the woman who was once Amish and is now running for her life. Micah was bitter after a tragic accident and survivor's guilt, but he's doing his best to raise his twin siblings.

Samantha has always walked in two

worlds—Amish and English. But she, like most of my heroes and heroines in this series, returns to Campton Creek to find safety and solitude. She wasn't expecting to fall for Micah and the twins.

I think this is how life works—sometimes we see God in our minds and feel Him in our hearts, but we're afraid to let Him in completely. We seek refuge in many places and in many ways, running toward that elusive dream of perfection. But as these stories have shown, life is not perfect. But God's love and the faith of family and friends can bring us that perfect peace of knowing we are not alone. I hope you've enjoyed this series and if you haven't read the other books, I hope you'll consider doing that. These stories have helped me through some bad seasons of life.

And who knows, you just might find me back in Campton Creek, seeking refuge again!

Until next time, may the angels watch over you. Always.

Lenora Worth